"The man has our secrets,"

Hawk told Carter during the briefing at AXE headquarters on Washington's Dupont Circle. "If he gets back to Moscow with that briefcase he'll be carrying, the Soviet computers will match up our technology with theirs. They'll be so far ahead we'll never have the time to catch up. It'll be all over in a very short while."

Carter didn't need to have it spelled out. An effective satellite program would insure the Russians of the ability to destroy every American intercontinental missile within seconds of firing. The bottom line?

We lose.

NICK CARTER IS IT!

FROM THE NICK CARTER
KILLMASTER SERIES

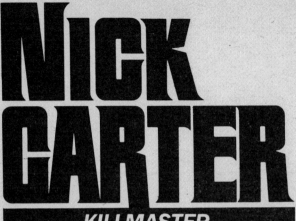

KILLMASTER

Last Flight to Moscow

CHARTER BOOKS, NEW YORK

LAST FLIGHT TO MOSCOW

A Charter Book/published by arrangement with
The Condé Nast Publications, Inc.

PRINTING HISTORY
Charter Original/June 1985

ISBN: 0-441-24089-5

Charter Books are published by The Berkley Publishing Group,
200 Madison Avenue, New York, New York 10016.
PRINTED IN THE UNITED STATES OF AMERICA

ONE

The tall, handsome man with the dark hair swept through the electrically-controlled doors of London's Heathrow Airport and rushed toward Aeroflot's ticket counter. He might have missed hearing the announcement concerning the flight to Moscow, perhaps even missed seeing the men in the cheap suits, if he hadn't run into the beautiful woman.

He ran into her. Literally. There were quick gasps as they realized in their mutual haste that collision was unavoidable. The woman raised her hands to ward off the hurtling, muscular body, but the gesture proved fruitless.

Nick Carter, late for the Moscow flight and angry at the driver who had brought him to the airport late, crashed through the almost dainty hands and into the soft, pliable body beyond. He had an instant's pleasure as he felt the full, heavy breasts against his rugged chest. Masculine and feminine thighs slapped together forcefully, then melded in an erotic liaison as the strangers continued the futile effort of avoiding contact. On Carter's part, the effort was sham; he loved the contact.

"Sorry," he said automatically as he reached out to keep the lovely woman from being knocked on her also lovely behind. He wondered, as he grasped her arms, if

1

she had felt the gun strapped under his left armpit. The woman was glaring at him. "Really, I am sorry. It's just that my driver made me late for a flight and—"

"Listen," the woman interrupted, pointing toward a speaker above their heads. "Is that your flight?"

The speaker was blaring: ". . . delayed due to mechanical problems. Aeroflot Flight One-three-nine to Moscow will depart at six o'clock P.M. and will leave from Gate Seventeen-A."

"That's the one," Carter told the woman, who was now showing a friendly interest in the muscular man who'd almost knocked her down. "If it had kept its original schedule, I would have missed it. Thanks for shutting me up in time to hear the announcement of the delay."

"You would have found out as soon as you got to the Aeroflot counter," the woman said. She smiled, but Carter was already looking at his watch, calculating whether he had time to buy this lovely lady a drink. He did. Flight 139 wouldn't be leaving for another two hours.

"True," Carter said, relaxing for the first time since he'd learned of the American who was departing on Flight 139. Stopping that man was vital, and he had thought he had blown it by being late. Now he had plenty of time— and he had an attractive woman who seemed willing to help him kill that time. "But you can still accept my apology and let me make amends by buying you a drink. Unless, of course, you have a flight of your own to catch."

"I'm also going to Moscow," she said. "And, yes, I'd like a drink."

Only then did Nick Carter detect a hint of an accent in the woman's mellow voice. And only as they moved down the wide concourse toward the main lounge did he spot the two men in the cheap suits. They were following Carter and the woman, walking only a few paces behind, making no effort to conceal the fact that they were watching the tall American man and the lovely woman with the hint of an accent.

In the lounge, Carter sat facing the door and wasn't surprised when the two men took a nearby table and sat so that they could stare at Carter and his companion. The men were too obvious, Carter decided, to be real KGB agents. The woman was another matter. He wanted to believe that the collision between them had been accidental, but he had learned during his years as a Killmaster for AXE, America's supersecret espionage agency, that few encounters were accidental when he was on the trail of a spy.

Nick Carter was being set up for something, but he didn't know just what. Not yet, anyway.

"You're Russian," he said to the woman when the drinks arrived.

"How astute," she said, smiling mischievously. "You're American."

"Bravo," he said, raising his glass in a mock toast. "And never the twain shall meet—except by accident."

She drank the toast and then looked at him with a melancholy gloom. "You must admit," she said in her fine voice that had so little accent that she could have been an American pretending to be a Russian, "our leaders don't go out of their way to encourage détente among the masses."

"They're afraid we might find something we like," Carter said. "What would happen to their fine war plans then?"

"Oh? We're planning a war?"

"Not us," Carter said, keeping his voice light and even

enjoying the banter with the pretty woman. "Our leaders. Left to our own devices, I rather imagine we'd just go on with the delightful practice of bumping into each other in airports all over the world."

"Nice that you can joke about it," the woman said. "I don't have that luxury. In case you haven't noticed, I'm being followed."

There it was, he decided, the lure to hook him on the prescribed line. The woman didn't know who Nick Carter was, but the Russians knew that American intelligence sources were onto the fact that a Soviet spy had been deep inside the U.S. program to launch satellites carrying laser and particle beam weaponry into space. The Russians had a similar program but were far behind the Americans in some highly strategic areas. With the data the spy had collected over the past several months, the Russians would be so far ahead of the U.S. that war—the final one—would be more than imminent, it would be unavoidable. And the Russians would win it, hands-(or missiles-) down.

Carter tried not to think of the war that might come if the spy got back to Russia with his briefcase full of vital data on the U.S. laser-satellite program. He thought only of how the spy had been tracked to this point only to be delayed by a mechanical failure on Flight 139.

The entire caper, Carter had learned in his briefing with David Hawk, chief of AXE, was typically Russian: brilliant in execution and resolution. The spy was John Parnell, a U.S. Air Force officer who, as a bomber pilot in Vietnam, had become disenchanted with American war tactics. Parnell had been reached years ago by KGB agents, had been trained in the Russian laser-satellite program, and had been instructed to worm his way deep into the American program.

This proved easier than even the Russians had expected. Within three years, the pilot had become a full colonel in the U.S. Air Force and was appointed operations officer for the firing of the U.S. "White Horse" particle beam prototype weapon at White Sands, New Mexico. He had been spotted only a month ago when he had been visited by a KGB agent eager to get a preview of his gathered data and to send some of it back to his bosses in Moscow. The KGB man had been under surveillance, and after he contacted Colonel John Parnell at the White Sands missile test site, so was Russia's key spy in the plan.

A check revealed that Colonel Parnell had worked in virtually every phase of laser beam and particle beam weaponry technology. A check of bases on which Parnell had been stationed revealed that top-secret files had been tampered with. The files were treated with chemicals that would reveal whether they had been photographed or photocopied. All had.

Then came a check of Colonel Parnell himself. His off-base apartment near White Sands was a virtual training camp for spying, Soviet style. Authorities didn't detain or question the turncoat colonel, but they watched his every move. When he flew to London and bought tickets on Aeroflot Flight 139 for Moscow, the President took charge of the operation, and Hawk became involved. When Hawk was involved, Nick Carter, designated N3 in the ranks of AXE agents worldwide, also was usually involved.

"The man has all our secrets," Hawk told Carter during the briefing at AXE headquarters on Washington's Dupont Circle. "If he gets back to Moscow with that briefcase he'll be carrying, the Soviet computers will match up our technology with theirs. They'll be so far ahead we'll never have the time to catch up. It'll be all over in a very short while.''

Carter didn't need to have it spelled out. Russian military leaders had been saying for years that when and if Russia achieved a significant edge on the U.S. in the race for military superiority in space, they would initiate a first nuclear strike. An effective satellite program would insure the Russians of the ability to destroy every American intercontinental missile within seconds of firing. The bottom line? The Russians could attack the United States or any of its allies, then destroy U.S. missiles the instant this country retaliated.

The mission to catch up with Colonel John Parnell and to retrieve that briefcase and its valuable contents seemed to have gone awry when the driver taking Carter from a downtown hotel to Heathrow Airport ran a police roadblock. British police were looking for a terrorist who had set off a bomb in a London department store. When Carter's driver, hired by agents Carter had never seen, ran the block, he guaranteed a police chase. Police stopped Carter's car two miles from the airport and detained him twenty minutes. Meanwhile, the time came for Flight 139 to depart. Carter arrived at the airport five minutes late and barged inside, hoping for a miracle.

The miracle was there, in the form of a beautiful woman with a trace of a Russian accent. Now, sitting with the woman named Andrea Boritsky in the main airport lounge, Nick Carter smelled a typical Soviet setup. The two men in cheap suits still watched them closely, and although the woman pretended that they were watching her for some mysterious reason, Carter knew that he was the target of their close scrutiny.

He hadn't figured out just why.

''Tell me about those two men, Andrea,'' Carter said as

he sipped his drink and lit up one of his custom-made cigarettes that had his initials embossed in gold on the filter. A cloud of aromatic Turkish tobacco smoke billowed around his head. "Why are they following you?"

"I don't suppose 'following' is the proper word," Andrea Boritsky replied. She was smoking a Russian cigarette. Its strong odor conflicted with Carter's expensive blend. "Actually, they're with me, watching me to make certain I get on the plane to Moscow."

"They think you want to defect?"

"Of course," Andrea said, glancing at the men and actually making a face at them. "My sister and I are dancers with a traveling folk group. A year ago, my sister defected when the company was in Stockholm. So they watch me more closely now."

"Where are the others in the folk group?" Carter asked, glancing around the lounge as though looking for women who looked like Andrea Boritsky.

"Performing at the Bigelow Theatre on Drury Lane," Andrea said casually. She took out a program booklet and slid it across the table to Carter. He glanced at it just long enough to confirm that the girl was telling the truth as far as it concerned the folk group and where it was performing. "I received word this morning," Andrea went on, "that my father is quite ill in Smolensk. I'm going home, but the KGB takes nothing for granted. They watch me to make certain that I do what I say I'm going to do."

The story was common, but good. Carter had no reason to suspect Andrea Boritsky of lying, yet he knew that she was. But why? He had run into her in his haste to get to the Aeroflot counter. He had asked her to have a drink with him. Why would she lie to him? How would the two KGB men or secret police in the cheap Russian suits be involved in anything more serious than a possible defection?

The answer came as a jolt. Carter knew. He was deliberately being deflected from his main target, Colonel John Parnell. He hadn't run into the woman; she had run into him.

All right, he thought to himself. *They're here to put me off the track, and so far I've fallen for it*. The question was, why? He had no answer to that question. But he had many more questions buzzing in his head. He decided to shut them off. He also decided to shake up this woman and her two followers.

"This is all very interesting, Andrea," he said as he blew out another cloud of smoke and put down his drink, "but I think you really should tell me the truth."

"The truth? You think I'm lying?"

"Of course."

"Then, what is the truth, Mr. Clever American?"

"The truth is what's in the briefcase carried by Colonel John Parnell, Mr. American Turncoat."

"I don't know what you're talking about," Andrea said. But Carter saw the grim set of her jaw and the thinning of her full lips. She was cringing inside, and she was frightened. Her fear was communicated to the two men at the adjacent table. Carter watched them start to rise.

"Sure you do," Carter said, deliberately loud. "You and your goony-looking friends there are keeping me entertained while Colonel John Parnell flies off to Moscow. Where is he, Andrea?"

The woman looked truly panicked now. The men at the nearby table were on their feet. Carter watched them from the corner of his eye, timing his next move to theirs.

"I don't know why you're acting like this," Andrea cried, her mellow voice cracking with near hysteria. "Who is this Colonel Parnell?"

Carter watched Andrea's face and saw the terror in it. He also watched the two men, and when they were almost at his table and one of them was waving frantically toward the door, Carter spun around. He went into a deep crouch and flicked his Luger from his underarm holster. The two men had been rushing toward him but peeled off at the sight of the Luger.

Beyond them, Carter saw two other men barging into the lounge with guns in their hands. These two were well dressed in expensive English suits. But they still had that Russian look on their wide, flat faces.

These men, Carter guessed, were the real KGB agents accompanying Colonel John Parnell. He had shaken up the woman and the two heavies, and the shaking up had brought the real pros out of the woodwork.

Carter aimed at the man on the right and squeezed Wilhelmina's trigger. The heavy Luger with the pet name barked in his hand and sent a deadly pellet of lead streaking through a thinning cloud of tobacco smoke.

Even as the first man was falling with a bloody hole in the side of his head, Carter was taking careful aim on the second. The two heavies, he sensed, had continued on through the lounge, out of the line of fire. Carter squeezed off another round and watched the second KGB man crumple with his hands clutching his chest. He wheeled around toward the table.

Andrea Boritsky was gone.

Wasting no time, Carter plowed his way through a gaggle of terrified customers and waiters. From behind, toward the main door, he heard the shrill squeal of a bobby's whistle. He had no more time for the police. He slammed into the kitchen door and rushed in, Wilhelmina still ready and hot and smoking.

Chefs and other kitchen workers turned weary looks in

his direction, as though sudden interruptions were becoming commonplace. Carter knew that the two ill-dressed agents and the Russian woman had fled through the kitchen. There seemed to be no help at hand, so he quickly picked out the doors leading from the kitchen. He started toward one at the rear.

"Not there, mate," a salad chef told him, motioning with a carrot toward a second exit. "The two blokes went out that one, and the lady took the one behind the main ovens over there."

Carter nodded and headed for the ovens. Andrea Boritsky, he decided, was his main ticket to Colonel Parnell. The two goons, he believed, had no knowledge of what was going down here. They'd been told to do a certain job, by the numbers, and they'd done it.

The door led to a corridor along which were offices for airport staff people. Carter bounded to the end of the corridor and found himself in a secondary concourse that led to Gates 1 through 30-A. He recalled that Aeroflot Flight 139 would depart from Gate 17-A; he hung a left and ran deeper into the concourse.

More questions poured into his mind as he ran toward the gate. Would the KGB have sufficient influence here to fake a delay in the flight, then sneak Colonel Parnell aboard? Had they arranged for the plane to take off while Carter was being the patsy for Andrea Boritsky and her two "followers"? Even more, if they had expected Carter—or anyone—to arrive at the airport, why wouldn't they just blow him away? Why set up an elaborate scheme with a "delayed" flight and a beautiful woman and two goons and two professionals, especially if they knew that the professionals might be killed in a shoot-out?

Nothing made sense here.

When Carter saw Andrea Boritsky and Colonel John

Parnell sitting calmly in the small waiting lounge at Gate 17-A, even less of what was happening made sense. They were the only people in the large waiting area.

And they seemed to be waiting only for Nick Carter.

TWO

"I don't know your name, sir, but you deserve a medal when you get back to Washington. You figured out our plan much sooner than we expected."

The American colonel sat with his legs crossed and his heavy body completely at ease. He was wearing a pale blue silk suit with a lemon-yellow Qiana shirt. His shoes, which Carter guessed had to cost in excess of three hundred dollars, were of rhinocerous hide, a material as illegal in African countries as was alligator in certain American states. Colonel John Parnell seemed content and perfectly in control of the situation.

Nick Carter sat opposite the man and his Russian lady, and decided he'd put a crimp in the colonel's style as soon as he learned a few more details of the so-called plan the colonel spoke of. As of that moment, he felt that he deserved no medals. In fact he hadn't the foggiest notion of what the plan was, except to keep him guessing.

"It wasn't difficult," Carter said, crossing his legs and lighting up another of his special cigarettes. "Andrea's story failed to touch my heart. And the goons supposed to be following her were far too obvious. I'll confess one thing, Colonel Parnell. I expected to find you with your precious briefcase in hand. I'm truly surprised that you'd

12

entrust it to anyone else, even one of your beloved Russian sidekicks.''

Parnell and Andrea exchanged swift glances, but not swift enough. Carter caught the looks and knew that he'd guessed wrong about something here. The American colonel thought Carter had figured out the plan. Now he knew that he hadn't. Carter had stumbled first, and the colonel had followed suit. Carter's mind worked quickly now, trying to figure out the part he'd missed.

The briefcase was the answer. If Parnell didn't have it, someone else did. And that someone, Carter guessed, wouldn't be at Heathrow Airport, not if the Russians had expected an American agent to show up at Heathrow.

Where, Carter's mind buzzed, could the briefcase be? He had to find out.

''Well,'' he said, spreading his hands as though to confess ignorance and ineptitude, ''I guess we all know where we stand now.''

''And just where is that?'' the colonel asked. Andrea, at his side, was more composed now. She had that small, mischievous smile back in place, and Carter felt a ping of conscience, knowing that the smile had suckered him for a few precious minutes. If it wasn't one thing, he thought, it was another.

''Obviously,'' Carter said, ''Andrea is one of your medals from your new Russian rulers. Nice prize there, Parnell. I hope it's worth giving up the best country in the world. Just as obviously, you and Andrea will take Flight One-thirty-nine when the KGB decides that it no longer has mechanical problems. Even more obviously, your briefcase with vital data in it is being funneled into Moscow by another route and another turncoat, or perhaps a Russian agent. I'd ask you what that route is, but I doubt that you'd tell me.''

Parnell and Andrea exchanged glances again. This time they smiled, and Andrea nodded. ''Why not?'' she said as she glanced at her watch. ''It's too late to stop him.''

Parnell nodded at the lovely woman, then looked at Carter. ''We had hoped to keep you guessing much longer,'' he said, ''but you figured things out quickly. Some things, anyway. Yes, I'm going to Russia now. My cover has been blown, but we knew that as soon as it happened. I arrived in London with a briefcase, but there was little more in it than a few sandwiches and a change of underwear.''

''Are you going the long way around to stall for time?'' Carter asked brusquely.

''No, not at all,'' Parnell said easily. ''There's no need to stall. Right now, one of our crack men is on the way to Amsterdam with the real briefcase. Our plan was to use me as a decoy to keep American agents busy here while the real goods were shipped out of Amsterdam. However, if you had missed Flight One-thirty-nine, as you almost did when you were stopped by London police, you might have tried to cover yourself by having all other European airports put under surveillance. Spies who fail have been known to go to incredible lengths to cover their mistakes.''

''So, when I didn't show up at flight time,'' Carter supplied, ''your new bosses cooked up the mechanical problems and the femme fatale bit to keep me occupied until your number-one ace got off on his flight to Amsterdam.''

''That is correct,'' the former U.S. Air Force officer said with a self-satisfied smile.

As Carter spoke his next words, his right hand moved inside his jacket for his Luger. ''I'm afraid I don't agree with your girlfriend, Parnell. Andrea's wrong when she says it's too late for me to stop the man in Amsterdam. With a few well-placed phone calls—''

''Put away the gun,'' a gruff voice said from behind Carter, who already had the Luger pointing directly at Parnell. ''You can shoot them both, if you wish, but you will die while you are doing the shooting.''

Carter noticed the perplexed look on the face of Colonel Parnell. The man apparently had considered himself important to the Russians. Now the truth was out; he was expendable. The news was easier for Andrea to digest— she had grown up under such logic. Carter turned slowly and saw the two men in the cheap suits standing a few feet from his chair. They were several feet apart, making it unlikely that Carter could gun them both down, even if he were the fastest shot on earth.

Another truth crashed home. These men were the true professionals. The men in the fine suits, the men Carter had blown away down in the main lounge, were the drones, the goons. *Christ, the Russians are getting more clever each day,* he thought. Then he added, *sure, they have good examples to follow in people like AXE agents.*

Carter's mind began a lightning-fast ticking off of possibilities. The two men were prepared for him to turn and fire. They expected it. Carter wouldn't turn and fire, but he couldn't hold onto the gun much longer and expect to stay alive. The men considered that Carter had only two possible outs: turn and fire, or drop the gun.

There was at least one more out. Carter went for it.

Just as a group of passengers came down the concourse from a gate farther on, creating a minor diversion and partially distracting the two KGB men, Nick Carter lunged toward Colonel John Parnell. He had no illusions about using the colonel as a hostage, but he wasn't beyond using him as a shield. The man had made his bargain with the other side, so let him reap the harvest that comes from such deals.

Carter heard sharp reports of an automatic pistol behind him. He also heard shouts from the concourse as passengers spotted the two men with blazing guns. And he heard grunts of pain from the American traitor as their bodies collided and Carter went flying past.

He came up beyond the now lifeless body of Colonel Parnell, Wilhelmina in his grip, and rapidly squeezed the trigger.

Andrea Boritsky screamed as a wildly spinning bullet from one of her comrades plunged into her chest. Carter felt a moment's remorse, but only a moment's. He had liked the woman and had even wished that her reasonably innocent story about the folk dance group and the sister who had defected were true. Now more lead was pouring into her as the KGB men tried to hit the squirming AXE agent.

Bullets from the Luger found their targets, and the firing stopped abruptly. Screams from the crowd continued and grew. Again, a police whistle squealed far down the concourse.

Nick Carter got up, brushed himself off, gave a quick, brisk motion as if to toast the lovely woman named Andrea, then ran from the bloody scene.

"Yes, sir, I've checked it out," Carter told his boss over the scrambled telephone line. "The plane makes a stop at Rotterdam in fifteen minutes. After twenty minutes on the ground, it'll head north for Amsterdam. There's a Russian named Anatoly Gritchkin on board and he's the likely one, although I won't rule out the possibility of a non-Russian name. But he'll need a Russian passport at some point, so my theory is that he's going Russian all the way. After all, it is an Aeroflot flight from Amsterdam.''

"And you expect me to sit here while you try to beat the plane to Amsterdam?'' Hawk demanded. Carter caught a visual image of his boss, gripping the receiver the way assassins grasped pistols, his heavy chin jutting out as he clamped his teeth down on a fat black cigar. "Why not just alert our man on the scene? He's five minutes from Schiphol Airport.''

"Because by military jet I can be in Amsterdam while the plane is still in Rotterdam,'' Carter said. "And because I'm the one fully briefed. Plus, I've got an emotional investment in this case.''

"You know what you can do with your emotional investment, N3,'' Hawk barked into the phone. "Okay, check with the airport manager at Heathrow. By the time he gets you and a chopper to the Fifth U.S.A.F. Detachment near Leeds, a Starfire will be ready.''

"Thank you, sir,'' Carter said, grinning into the mouthpiece. "I'll be in touch.''

Cramped in the small rear seat in the Starfire's cockpit, Nick Carter laid his plans for the time ahead. He hoped he'd get the job out of the way and check out the Nieuw Gudens nightclub in the Watergraafsmeer section along the wharves. Tammi Krisler was still the top-billed female vocalist there. He'd had good times with Tammi. Perhaps the good times could still roll.

However, Tammi had to be shifted to the back burner for now. Carter needed to review his plans for spotting and taking the man who called himself Anatoly Gritchkin. A man by that name had boarded Nederlands Airlines Flight 236 for Amsterdam, with a stopover at Rotterdam, just minutes before Carter had his impromptu shoot-out with the two KGB agents at Gate 17-A in Heathrow Airport.

He had reservations for Aeroflot Flight 9 out of Amsterdam for Moscow, leaving at 7:30 P.M., less than two hours away.

Anatoly Gritchkin wasn't the only Russian on the Nederlands flight, but he was the only Russian who was proceeding to Moscow. With luck, he wouldn't have been warned that things went sour for his side at Heathrow. All the Soviet principals had been killed, and by the time police got things sorted out, it should be all over in Amsterdam.

It was a cinch, Carter mused, that Gritchkin wouldn't be alone in Amsterdam. He had a fifty-minute wait for his Moscow flight. His KGB bosses wouldn't take the chance of leaving him alone with such incredibly important data in the briefcase owned by the late Colonel John Parnell. Carter would have to spot Gritchkin's KGB escort and separate the key spy from the outriders. Fifty minutes seemed like ample time to do this, but Carter had almost been burned in London when he'd thought he had plenty of time. He wouldn't let that happen again. Somehow he'd find a way to buy more time. Even though he would beat the commercial flight to Amsterdam with several minutes to spare, he needed all the time he could get.

Carter grinned there in the rear seat as he thought of how he'd buy time. The Russians themselves had given him the idea. He chuckled aloud.

"Beg pardon, sir?" the jet's pilot said through the intercom. "Did you say something?"

"Not a thing," Carter responded. "Just keep pouring on the machs. I can take all you got."

To Carter's amazement, the Starfire actually picked up speed. Even with a joke, he was gaining precious time.

The Starfire, its pilot pretending to have fuel pump problems, touched down at Schiphol at precisely 5:49,

giving Carter just a little more than half an hour before the
spy's flight landed, and much less than two hours before
his Moscow flight was to leave. It wasn't enough time to
take direct action and confront the spy and his escort. His
second plan, the one he'c copped from the Russians, had
to be executed.

"Stop on the tarmac opposite the Aeroflot hangars," he
told the pilot. "I'll disembark there."

"You've got to be joking," the pilot said. He knew his
passenger was an important man, but he didn't think God
Almighty could pull off such an unorthodox move. "It's
barely dark down there. If the Russians see you, they'll
shoot now and take their lumps, if any, later."

"It's dark enough," Carter said, gazing out at the
November sky and wishing he had an alternate plan on top
of his alternate plan. "Stop this fly-buggy."

"What excuse do I give the tower, sir?" the pilot
asked.

"The same excuse that got us here," Carter replied.
"The fuel pump that was giving you trouble just went
kaput. Cut your engine now. Make them send out a
mechanic while I hotfoot it over to Aeroflot and make like
a mechanic myself."

Carter climbed down from the wing and raced along
under its dark protection for several yards, then streaked
in a crouch for the distant hangars. Darkness was descend-
ing swiftly now, but he knew that from the proper angle he
could be seen against the bright western sky. He could
only hope that the armed guards that infested the Aeroflot
section of any European airport weren't standing at the
proper angle to catch a glimpse of him.

It was 6:02 when he reached the first hangar. He timed
the two guards walking their sentry posts and slipped
inside. He found a chubby, round-faced mechanic eating

his dinner at a messy, oil-streaked workbench.

"Good evening, comrade," Carter said in perfect Russian. "I must check the Saroya that is to become Flight Nine. Where is it?"

"Who are you?" the mechanic asked in Russian that Carter pegged as being strictly from the Ukraine. The Ukranians were at the bottom of the social ladder in the USSR.

"Stand up when you address a superior," Carter barked in his most sophisticated Muscovite accent. "And don't waste valuable time with foolish questions. Where is the Saroya?"

"It is there," the mechanic said, pointing to a plane. Then he leaped to his feet only to be tapped on the skull by the handle of a small instrument. While Carter had been talking to the man, he had flicked his stiletto into his hand. He didn't want to kill the innocent mechanic, so he used the hard handle to put him in dreamland.

Working swiftly, Carter carried the mechanic into a small toolroom and stripped him. He put on the man's coveralls, boots, and cap. They were far too large, but Carter didn't expect to be wearing them long. With the stiletto, which he affectionately called Hugo, he walked to the plane designated as Flight 9 to Moscow. He went aboard to find it empty. The mechanics and readying crew were on dinner break; apparently, all but the chubby one had gone to a mess hall or restaurant.

In the cockpit of the aircraft, Carter deftly opened selected panels and slid the sharp, needlelike blade of the stiletto inside. He loosened some wires and cut others. In one control box, he switched several wires that led to the engines' ignition system. With luck, the engines would blow sky high when the pilot and copilot tried to start them. At the very least, they would fail to start at all.

Moving back through the plane, Carter made judicious cuts here and there, effectively crippling the plane's guidance systems and its oxygen supplies. Even if the plane got off the ground, it would be like an eagle with a broken wing after a few minutes of flight. And the passengers and crew would most likely be unconscious from lack of oxygen before the plane went hopelessly out of control.

Satisfied with his work in the one aircraft, Carter still worried that the Russians would pull out of the trouble he and Hugo had caused them. He sought other Saroya aircraft in other hangars and resolutely disabled them in such a way that it would take all available Aeroflot mechanics several hours, perhaps even days, to make the planes flyable.

He had bought more time than he needed, but he'd learned overkill when it came to dealing with the Russians. They had invented overkill and they practiced it. Such thinking led him to a recollection of something Hawk had told him during his briefing for this mission:

"When the Russians get far ahead of us in the space war area, their first strike won't be merely to knock out a few strategic points in the U.S. or in our allies. We have it on good authority that some Soviet generals, madmen of course, hope to unleash as much as eighty percent of Russia's nuclear capacity. There'll be so many megatons of nuclear explosions on this old ball of sod that nothing outside the Eastern Bloc will walk, crawl, swim, or fly for the next thousand years, if at all."

That, Carter decided, was overkill to the max.

At 6:42 Nick Carter stood on the tarmac near the Nederlands Airlines section and watched Flight 236 touch down and taxi to its gate. He had disabled two other Aeroflot planes he had spotted empty at gates, just to make certain the KGB didn't commandeer them to stand in as Flight 9.

Then he had shucked the mechanic's garb and was in his comfortable tweed suit and trench coat—as out of place on the tarmac as a shark on a desert. He waited until the plane's engines had died, then he went inside the terminal building and took the elevator to the third floor for arriving flights.

He had no trouble spotting Anatoly Gritchkin. The heavyset man with the bulging eyes and the thatch of white hair was clutching the black briefcase as though it were a priceless and fragile antique. When he emerged from the boarding tunnel into the concourse, five men in expensive suits fell in step with him, two in front, two in back, and one alongside. The six men marched like an invading army toward the main concourse.

Carter had rented a car at the Amersfoort counter. He had insisted on a Volvo, one of the speediest and most manageable cars in Europe. Though he expected no car chases—in fact he despised them—he was still running on the logic of overkill.

After checking to make certain that the entourage had no further members lurking in the background, Carter fell into line behind the six Russians. He followed the six to the Aeroflot counter and lounged against a nearby pillar while the spy and his boys got the word.

"Sorry, Comrade Gritchkin," the ticket agent said. "Because of mechanical difficulties, Flight Nine is postponed indefinitely."

Gritchkin exploded. He cursed in four languages. He slammed the counter with both fists. Carter, who had seen Khrushchev beat a desk with his shoe at a United Nations General Assembly meeting, tried not to smile or grin behind the newspaper he had bought as part of his cover. It wasn't easy. When Gritchkin wound down, several of his comrades took up the battle.

The fight was to no avail. There were no available planes large enough to accommodate the flight, and no smaller ones that could make it much past the Polish border without refueling. If Mr. Gritchkin and his friends would kindly leave word where they could be reached, Aeroflot officials would be happy to notify them as soon as it was known when Flight 9 would depart.

This touched off another display of anger, then Gritchkin turned from the counter and marched determinedly toward the nearest door. He carried the black briefcase against his chest as though it alone could save him from the heartburn—or heart attack—the change in plans had brought on. One of the KGB men told the clerk that the party would stay at the Nederlands Hilton on Leidsestraat.

At the mention of the familiar hotel, Nick Carter closed his newspaper and moved toward a distant door, heading for the Volvo. He would see that the Russians were tucked in at the Hilton, then he would head out for the Nieuw Gudens and Tammi Krisler. He had done his job well, he thought.

But not well enough.

Instead of heading downtown toward the hotel, the Russians drove south on E-10, heading for Rotterdam, from whence the spy's plane had just left. At Rotterdam, Carter learned why the Russians were driving south and not north into Amsterdam as they had said they would.

The big black limousine that carried Gritchkin and his five bodyguards stopped at a filling station for gasoline. Carter stopped on the highway near the station and waited for them to leave. He drove in to query the attendant.

"Oh, you mean those crazy Russians?" the attendant said. "They're lost, that's what they are. The driver asked how to get to Brussels."

"What's so crazy about that?" Carter asked.

"The driver paid for the gasoline with a credit card," the attendant said. "I asked to see his driver's permit and he showed me. His address was in Brussels!"

Carter sat in the Volvo for a long time trying to decide whether to follow or to wait for them back in Amsterdam. He had no idea why they were going to Brussels, or even if they were going to return for the flight from Amsterdam to Moscow.

He knew only one thing. Somehow they had spotted him and were out to lead him into a trap.

Should he fall into it, or should he play his hunch that they'd return to Schiphol as the safest point of departure?

What the hell, he thought, and he fired up the Volvo and sped after the Russians in their black limousine.

THREE

For a man who detested car chases, the long night in late November was close to nightmarish for Nick Carter.

The Russians drove southward into the gloomy night, seemingly without purpose or set destination. Carter kept tight rein on the Volvo, hanging back as the chase led him through ancient and colorful small towns south of Rotterdam. The black limo continued through Ridderkerk, Zwijndrecht, 's-Gravendeel, Moerdijk, Zevenbergen and Prinsenbeck, then west to Bergen-op-Zoom, then south again through Woensdrecht, Hoogerheide, and St. Mariaburg and across the Belgian border into Antwerp.

In Antwerp, the limo pulled up in front of Chez Carlo, a nightclub notorious for its entertainment of the bizarre and kinky variety. Carter had been there on one occasion, years ago, and he'd hoped never to go back again. One act featured an Amazonal woman and—well, he shut off the thought and watched Gritchkin and his five playmates hop out of the car and go into the club. The driver with the Brussels address moved the car a block down the dark street and waited.

Carter also waited. After an hour had passed, he decided that he'd better cover his backside, just in case. The Russians could be in there savoring the porno acts, or they

25

could have slipped out a side door and could be on the way back to Amsterdam by now. Carter had become convinced that this trip to Belgium was what it seemed: a lark by a Russian spy who wanted to enjoy a final fling at what the West had to offer before his leaders destroyed it. He got out of the Volvo, stretched, checked his weaponry—including the tiny gas bomb taped near his testicles—and strolled casually to the entrance of Chez Carlo. The doorman gave him an appraising look as he approached. Carter slipped the man a hundred Dutch guilders and sailed on inside.

Christ, he thought as he gazed through the smoke-filled foyer into the club, *the Amazon and her two friends are still in business*. She was half naked and going for broke as she slithered and climbed around the back of one of the men. The crowd went wild. So did the man.

Carter nestled in a fake palm to single out his quarry. The Russians were near the small hardwood stage, drooling over the show. After twenty minutes, Carter left Chez Carlo and strolled down Avenue Braselle toward the black limo.

A mischievous thought occurred to him as he walked past the limousine. He thought of disposing of the driver and of taking his place, the way he had taken the chunky mechanic's place at the Aeroflot hangar. But he would have to kill the man, or certainly ruin his career, in order to pull it off. And for what purpose? he asked himself. The Russians were killing time until a plane was ready to take them to Moscow. Some arrangements certainly must have been made at Schiphol by the KGB to make certain that Anatoly Gritchkin didn't miss Flight 9 when it was ready. Perhaps the airline was to call Brussels, call the home of the limo driver. Hell, anything was possible.

Carter circled the block and returned to the Volvo. He'd wait there if it took all night.

His patience was rewarded in five more minutes. The Russians left the club got into the limo, and headed out of Antwerp on Belgium's version of the E-10 superhighway. Now Carter checked off the names and sights of small Belgian towns: Hoboken, Hemiksem, Schelle, Boom, Ramsdonk and Londerzeel.

In Brussels, the driver who was supposed to live in the city drove around as though lost. He finally stopped to ask directions, and Carter followed them to another famous Belgian nightclub, Chez Paul in the old canal section. Carter didn't go inside this time. He sat a block away in the green Volvo and watched the bored, yawning driver of the limo, and wondered if the man really did live here, and if he had a wife and children he longed to go home to.

The Russians didn't stay long at Chez Paul. Soon the limo was heading out on the eastbound highway toward Leuven. Carter was still recalling his own great times in lively Brussels as he followed the limousine toward Germany.

It was then that he began to doubt his assessment of the situation. The Russians could know that he was behind them and could be leading him a ring-around-the-rosy chase to confuse him or to lose him. Or, he now thought, they could be making a roundabout link with a connection that would help them sneak across the border into East Germany.

When the limo stopped in Leuven so that the Russians could get rid of some of the wine they'd consumed in Antwerp and Brussels, Carter checked his maps. Yes, the superhighway crossed back into the southern tip of the Netherlands and went through Maastricht. After crossing the narrow strip of the Netherlands that jutted down between Belgium and West Germany like a crooked finger, the Russians were a fairly straight shot through Aachen, Bonn, Frankfurt, and then the East German border.

Carter used the pit stop to good advantage. He found a public telephone, dialed in his code and had Hawk on the line.

"Sir, it's possible that the Russians have changed their minds and that the data we seek will be driven across the border into East Germany," Carter told his boss, speaking swiftly to preclude any interruptions and to conserve time—he had no idea of how long the Russians would be stopped, and he could not afford to lose their trail if his new hunch was right.

"You'd better explain it to me, N3," Hawk said grumpily. "We both know that the Russians hate to change game plans in the middle of a mission."

Carter told of how he'd sabotaged several Aeroflot aircraft to buy time, then had followed Gritchkin and his cronies. He concluded with: "I know you want to keep this low profile, sir, but I really think it's important to set up border checks in all the countries adjoining the East. Everyone should be stopped and searched. And . . ."

"You've flipped, N3," Hawk snapped. "The President would never go for border checks. He'd have to get permission from every government leader involved and that's hardly low profile."

"Yes sir, but I don't have to remind you of the seriousness of the situation if that data is taken into East Germany by car where a Soviet military aircraft could whisk the spy and his material straight to Moscow. I was going to add that perhaps you should have word of the border checks spread through Russian embassies throughout Europe. Gritchkin, I'm certain, is getting his orders from some

Soviet honcho located on this side of the Iron Curtain. If Gritchkin knows the border is closed, he'll have to return to Amsterdam and take his scheduled flight.''

"And you'll try to get on that flight?" Hawk asked.

"If I have to, yes."

Hawk sighed, complained, questioned Carter's sanity—all in a kind of good-natured grumpiness—but finally agreed.

At Aachen, West Germany, Carter knew that the plan had worked, and that the limousine had a telephone and a direct line to Gritchkin's boss. The limo turned north, reentering the lower portion of the Netherlands near Sittard.

It had become, Carter mused, a strange journey. Not counting time spent in nightclubs, they had been on the road less than two hours, yet they had passed through the greater part of the Netherlands, much of Belgium, back into the southern tip of the Netherlands, then made a brief sortie into West Germany. Now they were back in the Netherlands, heading north. In the U.S., they couldn't have passed through one state in that much traveling time. And in Russia, it took two hours just to get from one medium-size city to another. Europe was a small place in a large world. It only seemed big, Carter thought.

The Killmaster checked his wristwatch. He was now tracking the limousine through Roermond, a Dutch town of about 35,000 people at the northern end of the narrow section of the Netherlands that dipped down between Belgium and West Germany. They were, indeed, returning to Amsterdam and Carter was satisfied.

He was also bored. It was past midnight. More than five hours has passed since they had left Amsterdam. Carter didn't like to be bored. It was second only to car chases.

In his many years with AXE, Nick Carter had seldom

been bored. He had never liked killing, but there was something about danger and suspense and dedication to duty that had kept his juices flowing. A tall, muscular, clean-shaven man, he was a product of his training and his experience. As code designate N3 with AXE, he was the oldest agent in the organization. He had remained alive by keeping eternally vigilant, though he had done his share of drinking and carousing when the job or his whim called for such.

Nick Carter was a woman's man. When he worked, there was usually a woman in the background or on the sidelines and sometimes in the forefront. When he played, there was *always* a woman involved. He even wished that Andrea Boritsky, the woman he'd crashed into (or vice versa) at Schiphol Airport hadn't been so brainwashed that it led to her death. He wished she had been what she seemed, an attractive and available woman of the world. He wished also that she were right there in the Volvo with him, heading north toward Venlo.

Instead of a beautiful woman like Andrea Boritsky for company, Carter had a rock and roll station out of Düsseldorf and a series of yawns. It was while he was yawning for the umpteenth time that he became aware of a change in his situation.

He was directly behind the limousine. The driver had slowed as the cars approached Nijmegen, and Carter had been too engrossed in boredom to notice. The Russians in the car were peering back at him, and although they couldn't see his face in the glare of the Volvo's headlights, Carter knew that he had been made.

With a squeal of rubber, the limo pulled away.

"Dammit," Carter muttered. "A car chase it is."

He toyed with the idea of letting the Russians speed

away. He could always make a beeline back to Schiphol Airport and keep his eyes on Aeroflot flights.

But, the mere thought of the data in that briefcase held by Anatoly Gritchkin getting to Moscow made Carter's vital juices flow even more forcefully. He caught an image of nuclear holocaust for the West, including all the historic towns and cities he had driven through or past during this long ride to nowhere.

He jammed his foot on the Volvo's accelerator and again closed the distance between the two cars. Now that he'd been made, he had no reason to hang back.

In the cold early morning air, the two cars streaked down out of the low hills around Nijmegen and out onto the plains of the Gelderland in eastern Holland. The towns and their signs became blurs as the Russians and Carter increased speed over the flat highway. The cars zoomed through Oosterbeek and Veenendaal and Utrecht and Zuilen.

It was just north of Zuilen that a lumbering semi moved out onto the highway and cut Carter's Volvo off from the limousine. Carter cursed and sat on the horn, but the truck would neither move over nor pick up speed.

When Carter came to a long straight away and the truck driver finally yielded to the horn, Carter shot around the truck only to see empty highway ahead. He floored the accelerator and raced at a hundred and ten miles an hour until he reached the outskirts of Amsterdam. He spotted the black limo far ahead and decided to let the Russians think they had shaken him for good. He eased back and cruised toward the city.

Luck still rode with the Russians. At the Vanderfoort interchange, Carter saw what he thought was the black limousine getting off the superhighway. He took the exit ramp and spotted the car at the first intersection. It was a dark blue Chrysler, not a limousine. Carter cursed himself this time, and quickly got back onto the superhighway. When he caught up to the limousine again, he decided to draft it and let the Russians do what they wanted.

The Russians decided that they didn't want the American on their tail. The limo raced away with the Volvo in full pursuit. Just past the Vintergooten interchange, Carter saw the flashing red lights behind him and heard the familiar BAH-loop, BAH-loop, BAH-loop of the Dutch police siren. He filled the Volvo with profanity.

There was a way out. Carter could invoke diplomatic immunity, but he rarely did this, especially on a low-profile mission. His requests to have people stopped and searched at the borders to Iron Curtain countries would cause all sorts of howls as it was. These factors, plus his conviction that Gritchkin had no choice now but to return to Schiphol and await his Aeroflot plane, made him give in to the fates. Besides, he knew he had time to kill and he hoped he would be able to kill it with a very special person.

Carter thought he'd seen the last of the black limo and the Russians when the police car hailed him to the safety strip of the highway. The Russians kept on going while Carter ground to a stop, foiled by the highly efficient Dutch police. As the police officer was writing out a ticket, Carter glanced up to see the Russians in the black limo heading south across the center strip. By the time the policeman had instructed Carter to follow him to police headquarters and night court to pay his fine, the black limo was moving along north again, passing Carter and the police car at the correct rate of speed.

The flat, wide faces inside the limo were grinning. Carter was fuming.

The judge fined him five thousand guilders, which he didn't have with him. Destined to spend the rest of the night in jail, Carter asked to be able to make one call. His request was granted. He called the Nieuw Gudens nightclub and asked to speak to Tammi Krisler. She had left for the night, and since Carter could make only one call, he asked the club manager to contact Tammi and ask her to come bail him out. He had no real hope that the manager would call Tammi, or that the woman would come if called, so he settled down in his cell and began to calculate what he'd tell Hawk when this was all over.

Tammi arrived shortly after three in the morning, and she seemed happy to see the strange American who drifted in and out of her life for reasons she didn't quite understand. She suspected Carter worked for an American intelligence-gathering organization; she had seen his weapons and knew his style. What else would he do for a living? But Tammi Krisler, like most of the women in Nick Carter's life, rarely asked questions.

"You're a lifesaver," Carter said as they left the police station in the calm of early morning. "You're always a lifesaver."

"Somehow," the beautiful singer said with a deep sigh, "I feel that you would have managed on your own. Do you want to come to my house, Nicholas, or are you on a tight schedule?"

"Both," he said, smiling. "First, follow me to the airport, then I'll follow you to your house. In fact, this morning I'd follow you anywhere."

She returned his smile, which made her even more beautiful, and Carter felt an ache in his groin.

They went directly to the Volvo parked on the police lot, then drove to the airport.

At Schiphol, Carter did the only thing he knew he could

do. He was putting all his faith in the belief that Anatoly Gritchkin would take Flight 9 to Moscow when the plane was repaired and ready to make the flight. He would check the Nederlands Hilton, of course, but he didn't expect the Russians to go there after escaping from him on the highway. He had no desire to check other hotels; he needed a respite from the busy day and night, or he'd blow the whole assignment from exhaustion.

Nick Carter checked on Flight 9 at the Aeroflot counter, and learning that its departure time was still in doubt, he bought a ticket to Moscow.

Yes, he told himself as he returned to Tammi Krisler outside the terminal, he would take the same flight with Anatoly Gritchkin if he couldn't find another way to separate the man from the briefcase full of vital data.

With such high stakes in the pot, he'd follow the spy right into the heart of the Kremlin if he had to, and he'd fight every inch of the way to keep the Russians from gaining their superiority in space and pressing the buttons for that first nuclear strike.

"Now can we go to my house?" Tammi asked tiredly when Carter returned to the cars, illegally parked in a passenger loading zone.

"Now we can go to your house."

"How long before your plane leaves for Russia?"

He raised an eyebrow at her. "What makes you think I'm leaving on any plane to Russia?"

"You were at the Aeroflot counter," she said, inclining her head toward the ticketing section. "You gave the agent money, and he gave you something in an envelope. I know you're some kind of spy, Nicholas Carter, but I really didn't think you were one of *them*."

Only then did he detect the coldness in her voice and the rigidness of her lovely, supple body. She was democratic to the core, he knew, but he hadn't known the depth of her dislike of communism. He had to soothe her if he wanted the balance of the morning to be significantly better than the earlier part of it. And there was always the possibility, once he left her house, that she would turn him in if she thought he were a Russian spy.

Carter had given the Aeroflot agent Tammi Krisler's home telephone number so that he could be called there when Flight 9 was ready to depart. Tammi deserved some kind of explanation.

"My dear Tammi," he said, taking her soft hands in his and gazing fondly into her cool blue eyes, "you mustn't let your imagination rule your fine mind. I work for our side, the non-Communist side, but I can't give you any details. You know that from our previous meetings."

"At our previous meetings," Tammi said, her lovely lower lip stuck out in a pout, "I didn't see you buying tickets from a Russian airline. You know how I feel about those bastards, Nicholas."

"No, I don't," he said. "I do now, but I didn't before. Why do you hate them so much?"

"I am not Dutch," Tammi said. "I am German. I was born in Dresden, in what is now East Germany. My grandparents survived the firebombing by American airplanes, but I do not hate the Americans. My grandparents and most of my aunts and uncles did not survive the Russian army in 1945. The females were raped and the males were shot in the rubble by the Russians because they were outspoken in their devotion to democratic ideals. My parents, who were children then, were taken out of East Germany by Dutch army units and given to Dutch families. Two hundred children were taken out in this way. My parents, having so much in common, later married, and I am the sole product of that marriage. I have been taught to hate the Russians, but I did not need the instruction. It comes very naturally.''

"Believe me, Tammi," Carter said as he kissed her lightly on the cheek and savored her feminine scent. "I also detest what the Russian leaders stand for. I don't work for them, and if I can help it, I won't be taking a plane to the Soviet Union. You have to accept that on trust."

Tammi Krisler stood on the pavement and gazed up into Nick Carter's dark brown eyes. She saw honesty there, and strength and goodness and compassion. She believed him.

"Okay," she said finally. "Let's go to my house and get out of these clothes and this serious conversation."

"Not just yet," Carter said, remembering that he was going to check at the Hilton to make certain Gritchkin wasn't there. "You go on ahead. I know where you live. I'll be there ten minutes after you arrive."

"Where are you going first?"

He put his finger to her lips. She kissed the finger. "No questions," he said. "Faith, remember?"

"Yes," she said, kissing his cheek and moving swiftly away. "Faith. See you at my house."

Carter watched her go, admiring the movement of those sensuous hips and long legs. He wished he were following her, but there was one more piece of business to take care of before he would earn his rest and relaxation after his long day and night of effort.

FOUR

The Nederlands Hilton on Leidsestraat is a marvel of stainless steel, glass, and granite that stands as tall as any building in the city. The view of the magnificent harbor and the North Sea beyond is perhaps the best view available in all of Holland. To Nick Carter, the hotel was a gigantic stumbling block, a problem to be quickly solved and discarded.

Convinced that the Russians were billeted elsewhere, but determined to make absolutely certain, he marched to the main desk and inquired if an Anatoly Gritchkin were registered. The clerk checked on a computer terminal.

"Certainly, sir. He's in Suite Twenty-seven-thirty. It is quite late to be ringing his suite, though."

"No problem," Carter said. "It's one of his friends that I'm really looking for. I don't know the man's name, but he was with Mr. Gritchkin's party."

"Which man?" the clerk asked. "There were five when they checked in not more than two hours ago. See, here are their names."

Carter studied the screen. There was Gritchkin's name, followed by the names of his five bodyguards. One of the men, Boris Stanislav, was sharing Gritchkin's suite. The others occupied 2730A and 2730B, obviously adjoining rooms on the same side of the corridor.

"Thank you," Carter said. He turned and strolled toward the elevators. It seemed incredible that the Russians had gone to the Nederlands Hilton after all. They had to know that they had been followed on that ridiculous joyride through Holland and Belgium. Then again, perhaps they thought that the green Volvo had picked up their trail in the eastern Netherlands and had followed them to Amsterdam. Since the driver of the Volvo had been arrested for speeding—and the Russians had passed by to make certain of that—he certainly could not have known of their plans to stay at the Nederlands Hilton.

Then why drive such a long distance just to see a filthy porno show and a couple of nightclubs? Carter had spent much of his life trying to fathom what motivated Russians who frequented Western haunts. He hadn't succeeded, and he wasn't likely to figure it out now.

But he had a decision to make. He had to decide whether to make an attempt to retrieve Colonel John Parnell's briefcase with its valuable data now, or to wait and catch Gritchkin at the airport. The task wouldn't be easy in either place, but the hotel gave him a slight edge.

The Russians didn't know he was here, or they wouldn't have checked in under their real names.

The decision was made. Carter would storm Suite 2730 while the six men slept. If it proved that the Russians did suspect that he might locate Gritchkin and had put on extra guards, Carter had a second plan in mind. He would telephone Gritchkin's suite and pretend to be the ticket agent from Aeroflot. He would tell the spy that the plane was to leave in an hour, then he'd catch the Russians as they left the hotel.

First, though, he had to make certain they were up there

and learn if a frontal assault would be best. Although an assault on the thirtieth floor would be safest for innocent bystanders, it would be the most dangerous for Nick Carter. But then, when had he opted for the safest methods?

The elevator doors opened on the thirty-first floor, and Carter got off. He found the staircase door, opened it, and checked to make certain that it wasn't locked from the opposite side. It wasn't. He went down one flight, slowly opened the door a crack, and got the shock of his life.

The hallway on the thirtieth floor was full of armed men that Carter presumed to be Russians. In one swift glance, Carter counted twelve men, most of them with automatic rifles slung over their shoulders. He closed the door before he completed his count, knowing that there were at least another dozen elsewhere in the corridor. The men, wearing suits, topcoats, and hats, looked eerie in that hallway with their AK-47 rifles and their military bearing. Not one was slouched against a wall. Not one was smoking a cigarette. Not one was dozing on the job.

All were alert and ready for trouble.

Carter shelved both his plans, returned to his rented Volvo, and drove rapidly—but not too rapidly—out beautiful Amstelveense Weg to the Buitenveldert residential section. Tammi Krisler's house was quite large, set back from the boulevard among thick, high trees.

It would be a pleasure, he mused as he got out of the car and walked through the still morning darkness toward the house, to put killing aside for a time and spend that time with the soft and lovely Tammi Krisler.

Even as Nick Carter was being admitted to the house—and into the willing arms—of Tammi Krisler, a short, squat man in a cheap suit and a 1940-style fedora walked toward the ticket counter of Aeroflot at Schiphol

Airport. The man's name was Boris Stanislav, and he was in charge of the mission to bring Anatoly Gritchkin and his valuable briefcase back to Mother Russia.

Boris Stanislav had been worrying about the man in the Volvo for quite some time now, and although Gritchkin himself said there could be no possible danger from the man in the car that had followed them from the eastern Netherlands, Stanislav had the good sense to check out a hunch.

He had learned of what had happened at Heathrow Airport in London. Witnesses had told police of a tall, dark-haired man who moved with the speed of lightning and who had been firing a gun described as looking like a Luger. Stanislav felt no remorse for the deaths of the woman, the American colonel, or even his two comrades, men from his own section. He was concerned only about the man who had apparently caused all that trouble in London and had got away.

It was possible, Stanislav decided, that the man with the Luger was also the man in the Volvo. What was he doing in the eastern Netherlands? Simple, he had followed Gritchkin and Stanislav and their men there. The man had been on their tail from the moment they left Schiphol, but he had made his presence known only on the highway south of Nijmegen. Why he had done that, Stanislav had no idea. He had spent years trying to figure out what motivated American spies. He hadn't done it before now, so what made him think that he could do it in the small amount of time available to him?

Boris Stanislav was infuriated with Anatoly Gritchkin for taking them on the long trip through Belgium and the Netherlands. But the man was the white-haired boy in Moscow, and he had the briefcase containing the valuable data. If he also had kinky sexual tastes, who was Stanislav to object? Besides, Stanislav had sort of enjoyed what that girl did in that stupid nightclub in Antwerp. In all his travels through the West, he had never seen anything like it. Soon, he mused, there would be no West in which to travel, to eat and drink well, even to sleep with women who didn't spout ideologies.

After the performance in Antwerp, though, Stanislav had thought Gritchkin was ready to go back to Amsterdam. Oh no. Not him. He had insisted that the driver go to Brussels to continue the revelry. On the way, he had talked incessantly about the woman in Antwerp. Was the man crazy? Whatever his motives (and Stanislav also had trouble figuring out the motivations of his fellow Russians), the ridiculous trip had ended when the call had come from Amsterdam Command Center, notifying them that the borders were, in effect, closed; that anyone entering East Germany or any other Eastern Bloc country would be thoroughly searched. Stanislav had been happy, if only because it meant an end to the silly trip—and they hadn't really planned yet to use East Germany as an escape route. His happiness had turned to gloom when that green Volvo started following them closely just outside Nijmegen, and had raced them most of the way back to Amsterdam. He was only temporarily soothed when the man had been stopped by the police.

Determined to check out all possible options for a man who might be seeking Anatoly Gritchkin and his valuable data, Boris Stanislav could not sleep. He had waited until Gritchkin had gone to sleep, then he had slipped out alone, leaving a large contingent of armed men in the corridor to make certain the spy with the briefcase wasn't murdered in his sleep, or didn't do anything else foolish.

Stanislav strode boldly up to the Aeroflot ticket counter and rang the bell, since there was no one attending. A sleepy ticket agent came from the back room.

"Yes?" he said irritably.

"Save your snotty mood for the peasants," Stanislav barked at the agent. "Give me the list of persons who have purchased tickets for Flight Nine."

"I can't do that unless—"

"Unless you have a bullet up your ass, comrade?" Stanislav snarled as he hauled out an old .45 automatic he had carried since he was a rookie in Minsk. "It can be arranged. Now, show me the goddamned list!"

"Yes, comrade!"

Boris Stanislav studied the long list that revealed not only the names of ticket purchasers, but the time of day the purchases were made—along with a great deal more information required of Russian citizens. There were three Americans aboard, but two of them had made their reservations a week ago. The third, a Nicholas Carter from Washington, D.C., had bought his ticket a little past three o'clock this very morning. He had given no local address, but there was a local telephone number.

Stanislav would have no trouble locating the address that matched that telephone number. He hadn't been generous to certain individuals in the efficient Amsterdam police department for nothing.

"I will use your telephone," he told the ticket agent. "You will say nothing about this to anyone. I wasn't here, ever."

"No, comrade," the agent said with a tremor in his now polite voice. "I never saw you and this never happened."

"Right," Stanislav said, grinning inwardly. "Always remember that this never happened."

Carter remembered the big house well. As Tammi fixed

drinks, he sat in the overstuffed chair in the den and gazed around at the expensive decor. The vocalist had done well for herself, and even better since he was last here. He noticed some good paintings that he hadn't seen before, and the draperies were straight out of Charden House of London. He realized then just how long he had known Tammi Krisler. He had known her when she could barely afford chintz curtains for an apartment kitchen.

The stereo oozed a Gershwin tune through speakers that surrounded Carter in the cozy den. The colored lights above the bar swirled and swooped and added to his dreamy, lazy mood. The fire in the gigantic fireplace crackled and leaped. His feet on the soft ottoman felt good for the first time in days.

"Take a year off from whatever it is you do and stay here with me, Nicholas," Tammi said as she moved up beside his chair and slipped a drink into his hand. She bent low and her breasts touched his shoulder. He could see her nipples through her sweater; a great number of people paid dearly every night to see those breasts barely covered by a sequined gown and to hear the golden tones that came from her creamy white throat. "We like to live well, very well, and I can certainly afford to support us in the style to which we seem to have become accustomed."

"I'll have no woman supporting me," Carter said, sipping his drink and liking it. She knew how to please, that was for sure.

"Chauvinistic pig," she chided.

"You bet," Carter said, chuckling. He raised his head and nibbled at the softness of her neck. "Then again, you must realize that anything I say is negotiable. I may change my mind tomorrow and become a male feminist, if there is such a thing."

"You joke about serious matters," Tammi said, studying him intently. "I admire that facility. I wish I could joke about the Russians and about what happened in Dresden, but I can't. I see no humor in those beasts and what they are doing to this marvelous planet."

"There's humor in everything. It all depends on your point of view. I suppose the gods are sitting up in heaven, or wherever, laughing their heads off at our antics down here. If you were a god, wouldn't you laugh at us?"

"I suppose." She leaned down more and kissed him on the lips. She put aside her drink and settled herself in his lap. Her warm hand slipped inside his shirt. "Do you see anything funny about making love?"

"No," he said, enjoying the touch of her fingers on his hard, muscular chest.

"Then make love to me."

Carter got up from the chair and, in stocking feet, walked with Tammi up the wide staircase to her bedroom. He shucked his clothing in a formal dressing room off her bedroom, while she disrobed in the bathroom. When Carter was naked, he walked across the deep carpet to the bath. Tammi, her full breasts covered with soap bubbles, leaned out of the shower.

"Slowpoke," she said, drawling the American word like a Texan. "What kept you?"

"Three pounds of clothes and five pounds of toys," Carter said, smiling at her.

"I've seen those toys," Tammi said. "I'm surprised you don't want to keep them on while you make love to me."

"I would," Carter joked, "but I knew we were going to take a shower together as we always do, and I didn't want to get them wet. Every try to fire a rusty gun?"

"No, nor a *not* rusty gun," Tammi said. "I just hope the toy you *are* bringing to bed isn't rusty."

"Shameless hussy," Carter said as he slid back the glass panel and stepped into the shower. He admired her body again, as he always did, and loved the fine blondness of it. She was a true blond, from toe to head. The only bright color on the whole of her was confined to her nipples and her face. And the inviting pink of her nipples was every bit as delightful as the cool blue of her eyes, Carter thought.

They showered slowly, and Carter felt the kinks working their way out of his tired body. When they finally dried each other and he carried her to her enormous bed in the center of a great, pink bedroom where music also oozed, he was near exhaustion. She revived him, as she had many times before.

Seconds after they sank together into the soft mattress, Carter was over Tammi's body, first savoring her with his eyes, then dipping his head so that his tongue could tantalize the erect nipples. He felt the events and tension of the past several hours slide away. For now, he would put aside thoughts about what might happen if Gritchkin actually made it to Moscow with America's "White Horse" data. He immersed himself physically and mentally into the task at hand—and it was no task. It was pure pleasure.

"Oh, I love you, Nicholas Carter," Tammi cried when he entered her. "Even if you won't live with me, I'll take what I can get. Oh, and it's plenty, my love, just plenty."

For one fleeting instant, Carter thought of a future without AXE. He had lately pondered the advantages of a life in which he didn't face daily dangers and rigorous activities, a life in which the awesome responsibilities of world safety were on the shoulders of others. Such a life would be tempting to any man who had spent most of his days chasing or being chased, killing or trying not to be killed. Such a life with a woman like Tammi was doubly enticing.

The instant passed. Carter was back in his right mind, or in what he had grown to think of as his right mind. He was making love to Tammi in her spacious, comfortable house in the middle of Amsterdam's ritzy Buitenveldert section. He would not live with her and he would not quit his job with AXE. And in a matter of hours, the telephone would ring and he would go to the airport, fully prepared to take a flight to Moscow and get on with his assignment.

Aeroflot's Flight 9 was a death flight in every sense.

It could be death for Anatoly Gritchkin or Nick Carter, or both of them. It could be death for the whole Western world.

Everything depended on what happened in the next few hours.

The hell with that, Carter's mind nudged him. The important thing was what would happen in the next few moments. He plunged, literally and figuratively, into the pleasant pastime of making love to this beautiful, caring, adoring woman. His firm lips crushed against her soft mouth. He heard the low moans building in her throat and felt a surge of power through his belly and groin.

"Oh, Nicholas!" the woman exclaimed. "Oh, Nicholas, I love you, I love you, I love you. And Nick— oh, Nick, I can't talk . . . I—I—I—''

Sleep had come almost instantly. Carter barely had time to kiss Tammi good night before his eyes were sealed shut and he was snoring lightly. She sat in a chair and smoked one of his special cigarettes, though she rarely smoked, and stared at his profile in the gathering rays of dawn.

Nick Carter was the most exciting man she had ever known. She knew he cared for her, but she also realized that her own passionate longing for him would never be returned. A future with him in that elegant house was just a dream. But she had him now and that was sufficient. She would keep him as long as she could. Perhaps through this whole dawning day, perhaps for only a few more minutes.

Carter had told her that he was expecting an important call from Aeroflot. She had considered taking the call and not telling him the message. But that, she knew, would be the one way to surely lose this wonderful man forever. He had to do his job, and when he had done enough jobs and survived them all, perhaps he would remember a singer named Tammi Krisler, an East German girl brought up in Amsterdam. A girl who hated Russians more than anything in the world. In fact, Tammi mused as she thought over her conviction about the Russians, there was nothing else in the world that she really hated.

Tammi was a woman who loved. She didn't like to hate, and she blamed the Russians for that, for giving her reason to hate. Nick Carter, however, gave her every reason to love and none to hate. She would do anything for him.

As Tammi Krisler dozed in the chair and as the light outside turned from dull to light gray, a black limousine cruised down the street and stopped just past the big house. Five men got out.

FIVE

"Nicholas, there is someone outside. Nicholas, please wake up! There are men in the yard and one is crawling up—Nick!"

Tammi's voice came to him as in a dream that was quickly turning into a nightmare. Normally, Nick Carter needed only the snap of a twig or the cocking of a pistol hammer to bring him from deep sleep to instant alertness. But the toll on his energies the previous day had been great.

"Prowlers," he murmured, half asleep. "Anybody as wealthy and beautiful as you must have prowlers and peeping Toms galore. Go back to sleep."

"Nicholas!" Tammi cried, shaking his shoulder. "Prowlers and peeping Toms don't come at the crack of dawn. There are men with guns outside and they are coming inside one way or another."

That did it. *Men with guns.* Prowlers didn't carry guns, not in the open. Carter didn't know how they had tracked him here, but he had no doubt that the men were part of Anatoly Gritchkin's bodyguard contingent. He lunged from the bed and had grabbed Pierre when he heard glass shatter in a downstairs room.

Tammi started to scream, but Carter quickly had his

48

hand over her mouth. "Don't make a sound. This is a big house and we have the advantage. They don't know where we are." He laid the gas bomb on a dresser and put on his holster with Wilhelmina tucked inside.

"Who are they? What do they want?"

He saw no reason to lie. "They're Russian agents, KGB—and they're after me."

"Why?"

"It's complicated." He was slipping into his trousers when they heard a board squeak somewhere down below. Outside on the roof, something went scuttling down the tiles and crashed with a muffled sound on the ground below.

"Oh, my God!" Tammi cried. "They're all over the place!"

"That they are. Tammi, I want you to get into that dressing room and lock the door. It has no windows, so you'll be safe there. Please, don't even try to argue. We have no time." He was fully dressed now, his Luger and stiletto in place under his arm and on his forearm. He began ushering the lovely woman toward the dressing room. "I may have to mess up your house a little. With luck, nothing important will be destroyed."

"Oh, Nicholas, I'm so frightened . . ."

Carter turned her around and practically pushed her toward the door to the dressing room. "Hurry! And stay in the dressing room until I tell our callers we aren't interested in whatever it is they're selling."

"What *are* they selling, Nicholas?"

"Terror, then death. Get cracking, girl!" Even as he closed the door behind her, he heard stair treads squeak and knew that two heavy men were coming up. The man out on the roof was silent after having blown his cover by knocking a loose tile to the ground. That accounted for three men. Carter was thinking of the five men who had gone with Gritchkin on that crazy three-country ride. If they were assigned to him, then all five would likely be along on this mission.

With Tammi locked in the dressing room, Carter moved to a front window and surveyed the dark lawn below. The sky was brightening by the minute, but the copious trees on Tammi's lawn cast deep shadows and kept it predawn in the yard. Even so, Carter spotted a telltale cloud of smoke that could have been fog flowing gently out from behind a large elm tree. He watched, and sure enough, the man behind the tree leaned out for a quick glimpse of the house. He was looking for a signal from one of the men inside or the man on the roof. No signal was forthcoming, so he ducked back behind the tree and took another puff on his cigarette.

Carter scanned the rest of the yard and saw the next man—the fifth in the group—crouched behind the green Volvo in the driveway. The man himself was completely out of sight, but his brown shoes showed from beneath the front bumper in a kind of lump that Carter knew was not a part of the automobile.

He made a quick decision to take the man on the roof first. He recalled on a previous trip to Tammi's house that she had a large attic. He found the narrow staircase leading to it and went up, Luger in hand. The attic was empty, but there were tiny windows in the dormers. Carter went to the one nearest the area where they'd heard the loose tile scuttle down. He slid up the window and looked out. The side and back yards were clear of KGB agents. Carter was certain he had made the locations of all the men, and that the kill party consisted of the five who had gone joyriding with Gritchkin last night.

Carter eased out onto the roof and peered around the

dormer toward the peak. He saw the Russian's hands on the ridge tiles and knew that the man was lying on his stomach on the opposite slope of roof. The man was still keeping a low profile after his goof with the tile. Carter moved slowly up the roof, his dark eyes constantly on the hands that gripped the ridge tile ten feet above.

He stopped five feet short of the peak and put away the Luger. Silence was necessary unless he wanted the other four to zero in on him up there. He flicked the stiletto into his right hand and went the remaining five feet. He sat on the smooth tiles just below the ridge.

"Is that you, Comrade Stanislav?" he whispered in excellent Muscovite Russian.

"No, I'm Krumpinsky," the man whispered back. "Are you Salizar?"

"Yes. Lie still. I'm coming over."

"Watch out for loose tiles," Krumpinsky said hoarsely and contritely. "I found a loose one with my foot and I suppose you heard the results."

"I heard."

Now that the man was off his guard, Carter slid over the ridge as swiftly as he could, his back to Krumpinsky. Once he was beside the man, he swung with the stiletto and caught Krumpinsky a lethal blow just below his rib cage. The sharp blade punctured a kidney, and Carter twisted the needlelike instrument brutally to make certain the man didn't linger in pain.

Krumpinsky died with a soft moan on his lips. When his body went slack and his hands released their grip on the ridge, Carter pinned him to the roof with strong arms, then eased him down to where two sections of roof angled together. He settled the dead KGB agent in the crotch of the roof, then retraced his steps to the attic window.

Returning to the second floor, Carter saw one man

sneaking into the master bedroom where he'd made marvelous love so recently with Tammi Krisler. And Tammi was locked in the dressing room inside that bedroom. If the KGB man, whom Carter recognized from the airport, shot off the lock, Tammi would be easy pickings.

Carter had to avoid that. He was kneeling and taking aim on the man when he caught movement from his left. The second man who had come through the downstairs window after breaking it was now emerging from a spare bedroom. The man saw Carter and raised his weapon. Carter had no choice now but to let the man at Tammi's door go. He swung around and shot the man on his left. The man fired his revolver at the same time but missed.

The twin booms of the heavy Luger and the revolver in the confined space was like a bomb thrown into a sealed vault. The man fell, clutching his chest where the 9mm slug had crashed through muscles and bones and into his heart. He rolled to his back, and blood pumped in a gusher up through his shirt.

Carter was already looking down the long corridor. The man who had been at Tammi's door was gone. Carter knew he had gone inside the bedroom. He had to bring him out of there before the two outside men came barging in. Unless they were deaf, the sound of Wilhelmina alone must have set them in action. In fact, Carter mused, the sound of the Luger must have awakened the whole neighborhood. Soon, he guessed, he'd hear the irritating siren of a Dutch police car. Surely a neighbor would call the police.

For now, the silence in the house seemed deafening to Carter. He listened for the men to come in from outside, but heard no activity downstairs. He listened for sounds from Tammi's bedroom. Nothing there. He went slowly down the hall, inching along the wall, the Luger going ahead in his strong grip.

Time was leaping at him now. He had to flush the KGB man out of Tammi's room before the man discovered the locked dressing room and before the outside men became inside men. Yet he couldn't rush. His only chance was to surprise the man in Tammi's room. The Russian wouldn't know for certain whether his own man or the American were dead out in the corridor. He'd have to opt for the worst, though, and that meant he was now seeking a hiding place in the big pink bedroom.

The only hiding place was the dressing room.

Carter heard the crack of a small-caliber pistol and Tammi Krisler's scream as one sound, much like the twin reports of his Luger and the dead man's revolver. He ran the remaining few yards to her door, but the KGB agent had already pushed open the door to the dressing room and was inside.

Sickened by his failure to protect the woman, Carter moved into the room and took up station behind a heavy bureau opposite the dressing room door.

"It has to be you, Stanislav," Carter shouted toward the door with the shattered lock. "And you have to come out sooner or later."

"Not really," Stanislav replied in a cool, calculating voice. "I know you hit Salizar, Mr. Carter, but I still have two men outside and one on the roof. I can wait you out. If not, I'll kill the woman as soon as you show yourself in the doorway."

"Don't hold your breath waiting for me to do that," Carter said, emphasizing the part about holding breath and hoping that Tammi would get the message. She had once asked about the gas bomb, and he had explained how it contained a small amount of quick-acting chemical that killed instantly, like cyanide. He also said that he'd used it in situations where his victims suspected nothing, and that he'd had to take a deep breath just before releasing the gas. Tammi, a singer, had boasted about how she could hold her breath longer than anyone she knew.

"Do what you have to, Nicholas," Tammi cried out. "Don't give this maniac a chance to hurt you. Do what you *know* you have to do."

Carter heard the front door bursting open. Glass and wood splintered as the two men from outside finally decided they had to storm the house to protect their three comrades. He was losing precious time with each tick of the clock. He fished Pierre from his jacket pocket where he had put it after deciding not to tape it to his thigh. Tammi had given him the signal he wanted, by emphasizing the word "know" when she'd told him "Do what you *know* you have to do." He pulled the pin on the tiny bomb and lobbed Pierre through the open doorway of the dressing room.

Then, praying that Tammi would make good on her boast to hold her breath longer than anyone else, he left the bedroom and headed for the main staircase. Unwilling to engage in a running gun battle with the two outside agents, he waited until they bounded up the steps, then potted each of them with well-aimed shots from the Luger. The booms resounded through the house. One of the agents took a hunk of hurtling lead in his left temple. The second had opened his mouth to shout a warning. The slug plunged into that open mouth and blew blood and flesh out in a red halo around the back of his head. Both men tumbled all the way back down the stairs.

Carter raced back to the bedroom to find Tammi walking out of the room, her cheeks puffed out, her ample breasts more ample than usual. She had filled her lungs with clean air a split second before the gas bomb went off, and while Boris Stanislav had still been trying to figure out what the object was that the elusive Mr. Carter had tossed into the dressing room, Tammi had walked out. She pointed toward the dressing room.

"He is dead," she said, letting out her breath in an explosion, "but I wouldn't try to verify it just now. That place is blue with chemicals. What is that stuff? My eyes are burning."

"You can bet on one thing," Carter said, smiling at her. "It's not Chanel Number Five."

"Always jokes," she said. "What's the damage to my house? I suppose you and those stupid Russians tore the place apart while I was locked up in there. Do you have a joke to cover the damage?"

"Little damage, considering what happened here," Carter said. Then, hearing a whole cacophony of *BAH-loops* from police sirens, he began putting away his various weapons. "I'd like to stay and explain," he told Tammi, "but I've had my share of police. Don't forget to tell them about the body on the roof. If they ask who did it, tell them you were asleep when the shooting started and you haven't the faintest idea. They won't believe you, but what can they do?"

"To begin with," Tammi said drily, "they can put me in prison. Is that what you want?"

"No, but I don't want to see you incinerated, either. Don't blow it for me, Tammi. Just give them the lie and stick to it. I'll see you as soon as this is over and explain it all."

"Sure," she said, now looking at him as if ready to cry. She looked like a very scared little girl.

Carter took her in his arms and drew her close. The

BAH-loops were getting louder.

"Have I ever promised to come back immediately?"

"No."

"Have I ever broken any promise I've made?"

"No."

"All right. I promise to return as soon as I catch a certain man with a certain briefcase. It might be in a few hours, it might be in a few days. I might even have to go to Moscow, but I'll do what I have to do and I'll be back. Okay?"

"Oaky."

After a brief kiss, Carter left the house and drove away through a whole platoon of *BAH-looping* police cars.

Halfway downtown, Nick Carter had a brilliant idea that he could not have executed if he had stayed at Tammi Krisler's house. Undoubtedly, the police were all over that place by now. But he'd call her as soon as it was feasible and set the wheels in motion.

As far as he knew, the agent named Anatoly Gritchkin didn't get a good look at his face, and all five men who had been along on that crazy car ride were now dead. Carter could still board the flight to Moscow when it was finally ready.

He took a room at the Amsterdam Plaza under the name of Hans Vandergaard. In his room, he showered, then called the Aeroflot reservations counter to find out when Flight 9 would leave Schiphol. The flight was delayed indefinitely, the clerk said, so Carter gave his real name and canceled his original reservation. He would try again some other season, he said pleasantly.

Hanging up, he began to worry that he shouldn't have given his real name to the clerk. It was obvious that Stanislav had tracked him to Tammi's house through the airline, and he was certain that Stanislav had been trying vainly to mastermind Gritchkin's activities. Carter stopped worrying, recalling how Pierre's lethal caress had put Stanislav out of the picture.

But Carter was determined to be on that plane, not under his own name, but under the one he had concocted. He had only to place a call to Tammi when the time was right.

After a much-needed two-hour nap, Carter awoke, showered again, and made the call.

"Ja," Tammi's mellow voice responded.

"It's me," he said. "Are you alone?"

"Finally. You were right. They didn't believe me. But there's nothing they can do. I'm not going to jail."

"If you were," he said lightly, "you know I'd be there with a whole regiment to break you out. Tammi, I need another favor."

"Will my house get shot up again?"

"No. It only involves a phone call."

"Dammit. You mean I won't even get to see you?"

"Not this time. Will you do me the favor?"

"Nicholas Carter, after last night, how can you doubt that I will do anything in the world for you?"

"That's good to hear, Tammi. Now, listen carefully. I want you to do exactly as I tell you."

Tammi was silent as Carter spelled out what it was he wanted done. When he was finished, she took a deep breath and he could imagine those fine breasts filling out whatever she was wearing.

"Nicholas, you are absolutely and hopelessly insane," she protested. "I won't do it. I just won't!"

"You promised," he said. "If I must keep my promises, you must keep yours. Will you do it?"

There was another silence. This one ended when he

heard her let out a long-suppressed sob. "Oh, you know I'll do it, even if it means your death. And you will die, Nicholas. You're going on some suicide mission and I'll never see you again."

"Don't make any bets on that," Carter said.

He wished, as he hung up the telephone, that he felt half as optimistic as he'd sounded with Tammi.

SIX

The call from Aeroflot came shortly before noon. Carter had gone back to sleep in his hotel room and was dreaming of that long-delayed retirement to some quiet and remote place with a woman like Tammi Krisler. He reached out and snatched the phone from its cradle.

"Hans Vandergaard here," he said into the telephone. He almost blew it and gave his real name, remembering just in time the alias he'd told Tammi to use.

"Heer Vandergaard," the Aeroflot clerk said in terrible Dutch, "I hasten to advise you that Flight Nine from Amsterdam to Moscow will depart at precisely two thirty-seven P.M. today. The flight will have a brief layover in Warsaw and will arrive in Moscow at—"

"Warsaw?" Carter barked at the clerk. "Why is the plane stopping in Warsaw? I was told that Flight Nine was a direct one. I have business with your important military people and I am already much delayed. Why is the plane stopping in Warsaw?"

As Nick Carter, he really didn't give a damn where the plane stopped. In fact, any delay in reaching Moscow was to his advantage. But he had to play the role of Hans Vandergaard, president of a company that built a new prototype battle tank with nuclear capabilities. The com-

59

pany did not exist, but Carter had instructed Tammi to arrange a reservation for the nonexistent company's president, one Hans Vandergaard. She was to make it plain that her "boss" was an important Dutch businessman with key connections with the Kremlin, especially the Soviet military. Heer Vandergaard was going to Moscow to meet with members of the Soviet War Staff—all generals, so said the "secretary"—to discuss vital parts for the new tanks sold to the Soviets only months ago. Tammi had called Carter back to assure him that Aeroflot officials were considerably impressed with the importance of their new passenger.

It was doubtful, Carter thought, that any of the KGB men guarding Anatoly Gritchkin would suspect Heer Vandergaard of wanting to mess with their valuable agent and his valuable data.

"I'm so sorry, Heer Vandergaard," the ticket agent said, "but we still have several aircraft out of commission and must double up on services. We have many important passengers such as yourself who wish to go to Warsaw on equally important missions. We—"

"General Potemkin will know of this," Carter interrupted in a crisp, no-nonsense voice, picking a name out of distant memory. "But no matter. My driver will deliver me into your hands within the hour. I have no baggage, but I warn you that I will have many demands on your services. You will have a good Dutch wine aboard, I trust?"

"Oh, yes, sir. Will Hintergarteen 'seventy-six be suitable?"

"Sufficient," Carter said, sounding considerably bored. "A good wine, but a common year. I suppose it will do if you don't have the 'seventy-five. Ah, now there was a year. It would be worth three hundred guilders to me if I had some Hintergarteen 'seventy-five to accompany me on the flight, especially if we must spend time in dull Warsaw.''

"You shall have it," the ticket agent said gleefully, already counting the bribe that would go into the account to keep him in fine style when he defected. "If there is a bottle in all of Amsterdam, it will be aboard that flight with the name of Hans Vandergaard on it.''

"Thank you. My driver, who is also my secretary and factotum, will call on you before the flight departs. Your name, please?''

The agent happily gave his name and Carter committed it to memory. He'd have Tammi carry through on the bribe, in case there were questions after the plane left Amsterdam. He had to make certain that Gritchkin or his minions wouldn't tumble to him again.

After he had hung up, Carter called Tammi. "Can you be here in twenty minutes? The plan is working. The plane leaves at two thirty-seven.''

"Oh, Nicholas," Tammi objected, "getting the reservation for you was one thing, but must I drive you to your death? Can't you spare me that?''

"I could take a taxi," he said nonchalantly, "but it wouldn't be in the proper style of a big Dutch businessman with Kremlin contacts. Plus, it would deny me the opportunity to kiss those beautiful lips just one more time.''

"You are cruel," she said. "You know just where to strike your blows, don't you?''

"Of course. That's why I've survived all these years.''

"All right. Twenty minutes.''

Carter spent the time rearranging his weaponry. The officials at Schiphol weren't all that careful about inspecting personal belongings of passengers boarding international flights, but the people who ran Aeroflot were sticklers for every tiny detail. Most of these people, Carter knew, were KGB or trained by the KGB. Passengers weren't searched (at least, non-Soviet passengers weren't), but each item of their personal belongings was scrutinized, fluoroscoped, X-rayed, and turned, as Clint Eastwood would say, every which way but loose.

Carter took the Luger apart and packaged it into a special electric shaver, with the grip and clip in the battery compartment and the barrel alongside the coil. The stiletto, in its slender chamois sheath, was slipped into the lining of an expensive-looking pair of boots. The lining was itself lined with a thin lead film that absorbed and diffused any fluoroscope or X-ray image so that the section where the stiletto was kept looked the same as any other flat section. One gas bomb and one spare were carefully covered with a plastic material saturated with the essence of mothballs and placed inside an expensive wool sweater in a small carry-on bag. In fact, all of Carter's belongings were in the carry-on. His pockets contained only his papers, money (he'd received a hit from AXE through a local front organization, the same front that had provided Carter a driver at the start of the mission), cigarettes, and lighter. For the duration of the mission, Carter had given up his special cigarettes in favor of a Dutch brand that tasted and smelled, to Carter, like a burning tar pit.

As ready as he'd ever be, Carter bade the room good-bye and went down to the lobby. He wore a sedate gray wool suit and a homburg. His shoes, socks, shirt, and underwear were all Dutch, purchased in a shop two blocks from the hotel just before he'd taken his last fling at sleep. The graying mustache that graced his upper lip looked typically Dutch, but Carter had carried small artifacts like that around for years. He had thought of adding a Meer-shaum pipe and cane but had decided that they would be just *too* Dutch, plus the fact that he couldn't stand smoking a pipe. He planned to do a lot of smoking on this flight, if only to keep his hands from shaking.

Nick Carter's hands rarely shook, and he didn't expect them to shake while he was on Flight 9. But he would be heading into the heart of the Soviet Union on the trail of a spy who carried the fate of the entire planet in a small black briefcase. The importance of that briefcase was obvious to the Soviets, just as its importance was obvious to the Americans. Anatoly Gritchkin, in spite of his kinky sexual interests, was a top man, as had been Boris Stanislav. And on the other side of the fence, Nick Carter, AXE agent N3, was hardly to be considered a slouch.

For this one, Carter thought the two sides had chosen their best men from their best organizations. AXE was so supersecret in the U.S. that only a handful of people—if that many—in the other espionage or intelligence-gathering agencies even knew of it. On the other hand, AXE agents, or certainly their chief, knew the inner workings of every other agency functioning in or out of the United States. Even so, his time on Flight 9 would be nervous time, and he wanted something with which to occupy his hands.

There was only one flaw in his plan, he thought as he waited for Tammi to show up. The flaw, and Carter felt it was unlikely to happen, was the possibility that Anatoly Gritchkin might not take Flight 9. If so, he would already be on his way to another European airport.

Carter doubted that the agent had left Amsterdam, even though his checks of the Nederlands Hilton hadn't been conclusive. The clerk there assured him that Heer Gritchkin and his companions had not checked out and had not been seen in the lobby, but that was hardly proof that the man was there.

In his gut, though, Carter was certain that Gritchkin

would take Flight 9. The man was an egotist, considering himself infallible. Even though he had been followed and even though his five original companions who met him after his flight from London had been killed, he would insist that he was in no danger. After all, he had a couple of dozen more KGB men around him; what could possibly go wrong?

Gritchkin, he was reasonably certain, would indeed be on Flight 9.

"Smile, lovely lady," Carter said as Tammi drove her big Mercedes out the lovely boulevard of Overtoom toward the superhighway to Schiphol. "You look as though you're going to your best friend's funeral."

"Not just going to it," Tammi said, biting her lower lip and concentrating on the road ahead, "taking him to it. This is insane, Nicholas."

"I know. This is an insane world, Tammi. I'm just doing what seems to come naturally to today's version of homo sapiens."

"Won't you at least tell me what it's all about?" Tammi begged. "Don't I have your trust? Have I done anything to show that I might betray you?"

"You have all my trust," Carter said, his grin fading. "But I've trusted others who have betrayed me. No, you've done nothing to show that you're one of those, but it's best that you don't know more than you already do. If you're detained by any Russian agents and they learn of your East German connection, they could sweat anything they want to out of you."

"How could they do that?"

"You must have family members still in Dresden," Carter said, considering the usual way in which the Soviets got East German defectors to cooperate. "They could threaten to do them great harm."

"There is no one," Tammi said sadly. "I told you, I am an orphan."

"You also said that *most* of your aunts and uncles were killed," Carter reminded her. "That means that some were left alive."

"If there are," Tammi said, "I don't know of them."

"The Russians know," Carter said grimly. "If any relative is alive, they'll tell you of him or her, then use them to get you to talk."

Tammi pondered what he was saying. She had thought she had put her German life behind her. She had believed for years that nothing about Dresden could affect her so deeply again. But the mere thought that a relative remained there alive was an enchanting, breathtaking idea. Could it be possible?

"You're right, Nicholas," she said. "Even if they lied to me and said that I had an uncle or an aunt, or even a cousin, alive in Dresden, I would do most anything they asked. Don't tell me why you're committing suicide like this. I might say something to hasten your death, and I could never live with that knowledge."

"You're a remarkable woman, Tammi."

"Thank you," she said, her voice sad again. "I'll file the memory of those words along with the memories of last night."

Carter reached over and gently smoothed her hair behind her ear. It was like the finest silk.

"And you will come back from this trip?"

"Absolutely. You can count on it."

"But I won't bet on it," she said, chuckling softly deep in her lovely throat. "After what you and those men did to my house this morning, I can't afford to bet on lost causes."

"Don't count me out until it's over," Carter told her.

"Truth to tell, I'm a little nervous about this one. I'm going to beard the lion in its own den, and that's frightening.''

"You're not telling me anything new, my love.''

They made a curious and unlikely sight at the airport: the staid, conservative Dutchman kissing the voluptuous nightclub singer. Passersby smiled at them and seemed to think that they were viewing another case of the stuffy businessman being enamored by his lovely young secretary. It was precisely the image Carter wanted to project.

"Don't forget to give the man the three hundred guilders,'' he said as he strode toward the gate from which Aeroflot Flight 9 would finally depart. "His name is Pushkin, if you can believe that.''

"After last night,'' Tammi said, "I can believe anything. Good-bye, my love.''

Carter, as Hans Vandergaard, went through the security check with no trouble. He kept his eyes peeled for Gritchkin and his new entourage and wasn't disappointed. Ahead, at the prescribed gate, he saw the agent being taken aboard the plane in advance of the boarding time. With him were two KGB men with telltale bulges under their suit jackets. Gritchkin wasn't armed; he carried only the black briefcase, and he had it clasped to his flabby bosom. He was smiling as though certain he was flying home to a hero's welcome, the Order of Lenin, and a *dacha* on the Black Sea. He probably was, Carter thought, unless something happened on the way.

Carter would make certain that that something would happen, in spades.

Carter, as Hans Vandergaard, made strong, blustery protests when the Soviets checked his personal belongings and made him empty his pockets before boarding the flight. His booming voice and sharp comments in Dutch were heard up and down the secondary concourse, causing other passengers to turn and smile. They, too, were familiar with Aeroflot's policy of personal search.

As he'd expected, though, his weaponry wasn't detected by the special detecting devices that included a dog sniffing his carry-on bag for the smell of gunpowder. Carter had put the Luger's cartridges in a special, flexible, stainless-steel tube and had inserted that tube up his rectum, the way prisoners hid valuables from guards.

"You may go aboard, Heer Vandergaard," the official finally said.

"I should hope so," Carter snapped at him. "General Potemkin will hear of this disgusting display of ill manners, you may count on that."

"Yes, sir," the low-level KGB man said with thin patience. "I will await word from the general and will offer my apologies as I apologize to you for the inconvenience. Now, please board the aircraft, Heer Vandergaard. Others are waiting and the flight has been too long delayed as it is."

Carter snatched his carry-on bag from the official and stalked onto the plane. A grinning steward offered to take the bag, but Carter clasped it to his chest the way Gritchkin carried the lethal briefcase. He gave the steward his boarding pass.

"Yes, Heer Vandergaard," the man said politely. "Seat three-A, near the front here. Your wine is being chilled, I'm told, and—"

"Chilled!" Carter boomed at the man. "My God, man, you don't chill Hintergarteen. Never. The bouquet will be crushed beyond recovery. The wine will be as foul and tasteless as that bilgewater served in Moscow restaurants. Get my wine off ice immediately and serve it to me when it has returned to room temperature."

As he spoke, he slipped the steward a wad of guilders,

assuring a proper response. The steward took his tirade, bowed, and went off to take the wine off ice. Carter marched to his seat, casually scanning the first class and tourist sections for signs of Gritchkin and his two latest bodyguards. They weren't in first class; of that he was certain. And he couldn't see the more than two hundred faces in tourist.

Mistake, Carter thought. Even though he was supposed to be an important Dutch tank builder, he should have flown tourist to keep an eye on Gritchkin. As important as the agent was, his bosses wouldn't spring for first class, partly because they didn't want the high visibility for him, partly because they were always watching the budget.

He would take his seat, but before the plane took off, he'd make a visit to the lavatory in the rear of the plane. He had to know where Gritchkin was sitting. Hell, he had to know that the man was even on the plane. Sure, he'd seen him and his two guards being ushered into the boarding tunnel, but he hadn't seen him actually enter the plane. The tunnel had an access door near the plane door; Gritchkin could have been sneaked out that door, down a ladder, and back inside the terminal.

The steward came to tell Heer Vandergaard that his precious wine had been taken off ice and put into a microwave oven to warm it.

"You're insane!" Carter exploded. "Microwaves kill everything of beauty in wine. Bouquet, body, taste. My God, I might as well dip my wineglass in your chemical toilet as drink wine that has been subjected to microwaves. Have you lost all your wits?"

Carter listened to the man's further apologies and decided he'd done enough blustering and complaining. He was disliked by most of the other passengers by now, and considered the last man aboard to be a Western spy. His cover was solid. He had only to determine where Gritchkin sat and polish up his plans to separate the man from his bodyguards and that precious briefcase.

The plan was so simple that it had to work. Hans Vandergaard would have a kidney problem that required him to make frequent trips to the lavatory. On one of his passes, he would surely be jostled by air turbulence, and he would have the special chemical in hand to pour into whatever Gritchkin was drinking when he fell against the man's seat. The chemical would give the spy temporary kidney problems and send him flying to the lavatory every few minutes. The plan depended on Gritchkin having a drink of some sort, but the trip through Belgium and West Germany and back to Amsterdam had assured Carter that the man was a heavy drinker. The six Russians hadn't missed many watering holes during that drive.

Gritchkin would have a drink in his hand; Carter would make book on that.

Carter also wanted a drink in his hand, all part of his image as a hard-working, hard-drinking Dutch executive. He summond the steward and said that since the wine had been ruined, he'd settle for a scotch and short water. He sipped the drink, and when it was three minutes to takeoff and the engines had been started, he got up to go to the rear lavatory.

"Sorry, Heer Vandergaard," the ever-watchful steward told him. "You must remain seated with your belt fastened."

"It's a good custom," Carter agreed in his gruff Dutch voice, "but not when a man's bladder is about to burst. I cannot wait."

"But you must," the steward said firmly.

Carter was about to barge past the man, when a second steward, a tough-looking man who'd known KGB school many years ago and a lot of hard knocks (given and taken) since then, stepped from the tiny kitchen to support his comrade.

"You must return to your seat," the tough-looking stward said. "It is the rule."

Carter saw that several passengers were looking disgustedly at him.

To hell with them, he thought, but he wished the Soviet airline went for stewardesses, not stewards from KGB schools. But he had no choice; he dropped into his seat, sipped his scotch, and watched the airport buildings whiz past as the big Saroya streaked down the runway.

In seconds, Flight 9 to Moscow, with a stopover in Warsaw, was on its way.

As soon as the seat belt sign flicked off, Carter got up with his carry-on bag, nodded to the two stewards who were already beginning to prepare lunch, and went toward the rear. He went slowly, giving each face a casual glance. He saw Gritchkin's two guards first, sitting in a window and an aisle seat on the left, using the center seat for a game of cards. In the aisle seat behind, his face buried in a magazine, was Anatoly Gritchkin. The briefcase was on his lap.

There was a problem, though. The man had no drink.

Well, Carter would wait. With enough trips to the lavatory, his chance would come. All the pieces would fall into place. The drink would be there, and the turbulence would come as it always did when planes crossed the mountains of the German Rhineland and of western Poland.

Carter would make sure one of his trips to the lavatory coincided with one by the KGB agent, and he would pull him inside, kill him, destroy his data on America's White

Horse project, and take his chances on returning from Warsaw alive.

The Warsaw stopover was proving a godsend now. But the other parts had to come too. Carter began to sweat in the stuffy lavatory, thinking perhaps that they wouldn't come. He had planned well, but even good plans didn't always work out favorably.

He'd take one thing at a time. He sat on the toilet lid, opened his carry-on bag, and took out his electric shaver. He was reassembling the parts of his Luger when the door, which he had latched, suddenly opened. The tough-looking steward from the school of hard knocks stood there staring at him, an evil grin spreading across his wide, flat face.

In the steward's hand was an automatic pistol.

"Return to your seat, Heer Vandergaard," the steward commanded. "The pilot will have a word with you. I'll take that pistol you're assembling."

The man reached in for Carter's Luger.

SEVEN

It was the rugged steward's confidence that did him in. Carter read the man accurately and knew that the last thing the man expected from the Dutch businessman was aggression. Even though the steward, obviously a trained operative, must have been taught that attack was the best weapon of defense, he had apparently forgotten it in his joy over having caught an unsavory passenger assembling a weapon that had been smuggled aboard.

The steward, Carter guessed, was probably already thinking of the medal that would be pinned on him by no less than the president of Aeroflot, and perhaps even the chief of the KGB.

Carter snatched the outstretched hand and yanked the man inside. He closed and latched the door even as his hand was closing over the man's mouth to keep him from shouting for help. He brought the Luger down on the hard skull, felt the steward go slack, and tried to lower him to the floor. There was no room in the tiny lavatory for the man to lie on the floor. Carter propped him in a corner.

Working swiftly, he took the man's automatic pistol and slipped it down into his own jockey shorts, faintly shocked at its coldness against his private parts. He took a flask from his bag and poured some scotch into the steward's mouth, letting it spill over the front of his uniform. He checked the man's skull where he had cracked him with the side of Wilhelmina. There was no bump, no broken skin.

His story might hold up, it might not. He had no other choice.

For effect, Carter let out a loud exclamation of disgust. He whacked the side of the wall to make it sound as though someone had just fallen. He opened the door and bounded outside, complaining loudly in a combination of Dutch and Russian.

"Someone get the captain," he yelled. "One of the stewards is drunk and he barged in on me. He knew I had a flask and he demanded a drink and then he passed out. Call the captain!"

The pilot was soon there, and Carter, as Hans Vandergaard, explained again what had happened. The captain, who knew that the steward was KGB but who couldn't admit this openly, pretended to accept the story. He called two other stewards and told them to take the man to the cockpit where he could lie on the floor to sober up.

To lend greater credence to his story that the man was drunk, Carter had slipped him some of the chemical he'd reserved for Gritchkin. As the man was being carried up the aisle, he wet his trousers, to the utter disgust of passengers along the way. Even the captain began to doubt his assessment of the situation.

Back in his seat, Carter knew that his story would hold up only until the steward awoke. It could be a few minutes, or a half hour. Carter hoped for a half hour. By then, the plane would be in Warsaw. He'd have to have his work done before they reached Warsaw, or he'd be on this death flight right into the heart of Russia.

● ● ●

The first turbulence came as the plane approached the valley of the Rhine River. The low mountains there, along with the deep valley, combined to force treacherous air currents high into the sky. Carter was ready.

"Sorry," he said as he stumbled back through the aisle, bumping into seats and passengers alike. "Sorry for so many trips to the lavatory, but I have this kidney problem."

"He also has a mouth problem," a woman muttered in German to her companion.

"And a drinking one," the companion responded. "They ought to put him on the cockpit floor with the drunken steward. They deserve each other."

This trip to the lavatory served only to stir up passengers and make their dislike for the Dutch boor greater. Gritchkin still had no drink and showed no signs of needing to go to the toilet. Carter made his trip short and returned to his seat, disgusted with himself for not having an alternate plan, disgusted with the whole mission that hadn't gone right from the very beginning.

He hadn't anticipated the use of a decoy in the person of the real traitor, Colonel John Parnell. He hadn't anticipated a lot of things. He'd been so convinced that the KGB wouldn't check all possibilities that he'd used his own name when he'd first reserved space on this delayed flight. They'd traced him through that, and Tammi Krisler had nearly lost her life and her house as a result.

And now the steward was onto him, and although presently unconscious, he would come to shortly and spill his guts. As for Gritchkin, he wasn't running true to form. He had revealed his penchant for bizarre sex and plenty of booze during that night-long junket in the black limousine, yet now, aboard a plane home, he was playing the role of Paul Perfect.

Even the magazine he was reading, Carter had noticed,

was a *Tass* offshoot, full of top Communist dogma and articles written by members of the Presidium.

Suddenly the man had no weaknesses.

Ah, Carter thought, but airplanes did. They hadn't reached the halfway point to Warsaw yet. A mechanical problem would send Flight 9 kiting back to Schiphol.

The Killmaster was quickly on his feet, apologizing again for the inconvenience of so many trips to the lavatory as he bustled back through the aisle and into the little toilet. He removed a panel and found a relay switch box that led to controls for the rudder. He didn't want to do anything drastic, such as sending the big aircraft into a tailspin. He wanted only to make the controls mushy—a harbinger of big trouble ahead—enough to send the pilot into a 180-degree turn and a return to Amsterdam.

Using Hugo, which he'd taken from his boot lining, he shaved the insulation off two small wires. He separated the many strands of wire and began to snip them one by one. When each wire had only a few strands, he replaced the panel cover, flushed the toilet, and returned to his seat. Already the rear of the plane was beginning to yaw from side to side.

Carter was no sooner back in his seat when the sign lit up, in French, English, and Russian: FASTEN SEAT BELTS. And then the captain's voice blared through the intercom.

"We have received word that an important passenger missed the flight in Amsterdam," the captain lied. "We will be returning for him. The airline is sorry for any inconvenience, but this passenger is required in Moscow for an important meeting of Party members. We know that you will understand."

And the plane began a shaky, wobbly turn that soon set it on a westerly course, back over the Rhine valley and the turbulence waiting there. Carter only hoped that the turbulence wouldn't be enough to finish the job he'd begun on the rudder controls. Given his choice of ways to die, he'd much prefer going in a shoot-out with Anatoly Gritchkin than in a flaming crash in the Rhine valley.

Aeroflot Flight 9 was on the downwind leg of its approach to Runway 63 at Schiphol when the world started to fall apart once again for the AXE agent named Nick Carter. The flight engineer passed Carter's seat. He thought nothing of the visit to the passenger compartment by a member of the flight crew, and was thus unprepared for what happened next.

The cockpit door opened again, and the burly steward that Carter had coldcocked in the lavatory and accused of being dead drunk moved out. He had no gun, but the look on his face told Carter that he fully believed he really didn't need one.

The steward reached Carter's seat at the same time the flight engineer returned from the tourist section with the two KGB men who were accompanying Anatoly Gritchkin. The key man himself stood in the aisle a few seats back, watching Carter with bemused interest.

"Please come to the rear of the aircraft," the flight engineer said to Carter. "We wish to speak with you there."

"If you have anything to say to me," Carter said loudly in deliberately mangled Russian, "you can damned well say it here. I'll have you know that . . ."

The two KGB guards produced small revolvers that they pointed at Carter. Their faces revealed that they'd receive great pleasure in pulling the triggers of those revolvers. Carter arose, and with the flight engineer and the steward leading and the two KGB men and Gritchkin trailing. The party moved to the rear of the plane where there were several empty seats. The rear section, however, was yawing violently now as the pilot tried to land with mushy controls. The winds off the North Sea were wicked for landing aircraft at this time of year, even under the best of circumstances.

"You will remain here," the flight engineer told Carter, motioning to an empty seat. "When all the passengers have left, there are those who wish to ask a few questions."

Carter's only chance, he believed, lay in pretending to be what he looked like: a Dutch businessman on his way to sell the Russians some parts for tanks he'd sold them earlier.

"I am a citizen of the Netherlands," he said in Dutch. "If you persist in detaining me, you will answer to our police, our government and our Queen. Furthermore, I happen to be a personal friend of General Potemkin and am supposed to be meeting with him this very afternoon."

"I see," the flight engineer said. "And which General Potemkin is that? We have three by that name, so I'm informed."

"General Grigori Aleksandrovich Potemkin," Carter said. "He is the head of the Redstar Regiment in—"

"Not true," a voice from behind the KGB guards said. "The man you speak of is none other than a Russian field marshal who was a favorite of Empress Catherine, otherwise known as Catherine the Great. And he died with considerable aristocratic honors in 1791, nearly two hundred years ago. I would be interested in attending this meeting you speak of, if you should ever get to Moscow."

The guards had parted, and as the plane moved into its final approach, Carter found himself eyeball-to-eyeball with none other than Anatoly Gritchkin. The master spy still held the black briefcase. He was smiling at Carter and held a drink in his hand. Carter cursed under his breath at the sight of the drink. *Now he decides to have one*, he thought. *Jesus, what lousy timing*.

"Perhaps it can be arranged," Carter said to the agent. But there was no spark in his bravado now.

"And perhaps you can tell us who you are and what you are doing on this plane," Gritchkin said, the smile fading. "I'm told that you struck this steward on the head and took his weapon from him, then tried to convince the captain that he was an unruly drunk. I don't ask if this is true. I only ask who you are and what you are doing here."

To emphasize his remarks, Gritchkin reached out and ripped the phony mustache from Carter's upper lip. It would have hurt like hell, but Carter had been sweating so profusely that the glue used to hold the mustache in place was tacky and loose. In time, the damned thing would have slipped off on its own, Carter thought bitterly.

"I am Santa Claus," he said, returning Gritchkin's hard gaze, "and I want to get home as quickly as possible. Christmas is only a month off and those damned elves are useless when I'm not there to . . ."

The steward that Carter had knocked out slapped the AXE agent across the mouth. Carter tasted blood in his mouth an instant before a thin stream of it trickled down his chin.

"Give me the pistol you took from me," the steward demanded. "I want it now."

"I don't have your pistol."

The steward slapped him again, this time with his fist. Carter's head snapped back against the seat. Several passengers had turned to look back at what was happening. The two KGB guards scowled at them, and they resumed their positions facing the front of the plane.

"Give the man his pistol," Gritchkin ordered. "After that, you can answer my questions."

Carter undid his belt and reached in for the automatic weapon that was still in his shorts, and still cramping his style, though it was no longer cold.

"Bring it out by the barrel," Gritchkin said.

Carter nodded but closed his hand on the pistol's grip. A new and desperate plan was forming. The plane was still yawing and shaking violently as it approached touchdown. If he could delay for only a few seconds. . . .

"One moment," he muttered. "It's snagged on my trousers."

He pretended to struggle with the gun. The men around him prepared for a trick. Carter had no more tricks; he was depending on the aircraft and the work he'd done on the rudder controls to provide a new trick.

It came with an ear-shattering screech and a brutal thrashing about as the touchdown came and the rudder controls apparently could not do their normal job. The big rudder was flapping wildly, causing the plane to veer back and forth as it screamed down the runway.

Carter had been sitting; his interrogators had been standing. He had loaded the situation in his favor by quietly snapping his seat belt. When the retro jets were fired to slow the plane, the rudder lost it. The plane made a sharp, whipping turn to the left, then swung violently back to the right.

The flight engineer, the spy, the steward, and the KGB guards went sprawling in a heap into one set of seats, only to be thrown back across the aisle into the adjacent row.

Carter had the automatic pistol out in an instant. He saw that the steward had been only mildly dazed and was coming out of a seat after Carter. He squeezed the trigger, and the pistol chattered its sound of doom that was barely heard for the roar of the engines in retro.

In that moment, as the steward fell back with a bloody line stitched across his white shirt, the plane stopped yawing and veering. The passengers, who had broken into screams and cries, had forgotten the little drama at the rear of the plane. They had been hanging on for dear life and weren't convinced that the worst was over. Carter knew that it was, at least where the plane was concerned.

As for his future as a living member of the human race, he wasn't so sure.

With a quick scan of his brown eyes, he assessed his chances. The flight engineer and Gritchkin were unconscious, as was one of the KGB guards. The second guard was stirring but was still in a fog. Carter leaned over and tapped him hard behind the ear; the stirring stopped.

Carter wasted no time getting to Gritchkin, who was sprawled across three empty seats, his stubby legs in the aisle. The plane was slowing now and the yawing had stopped. The passengers were regaining composure, and some of them were looking at the men sprawled across the rear seats. A fat woman in a fur coat saw the blood on the steward's shirt and began screaming.

Carter ignored her and the others. He yanked Gritchkin off the seats and turned him over just as the plane left the main runway and headed for the gates. Carter lifted the agent's arms and saw that the briefcase was handcuffed to his right wrist.

"You! What are you doing?"

It was the steward who had chilled the wine and then had warmed it in the microwave oven. He was lurching down the aisle of the tourist section, gazing open-mouthed at what looked like a massacre. When he saw the blood on his coworker's shirt, he gasped and stopped.

"On the floor!" Carter ordered, waving the automatic pistol. "Just lie on your stomach and nothing will happen to you."

"A skyjacking?" the steward said, aghast. "Nobody

has ever skyjacked a Russian plane before. You—''

''I said, on the floor!''

The man hit the deck and covered his head with his hands. Carter turned back to the briefcase. It was locked. He drew back the automatic pistol, wishing he had his Luger operative, and prepared to blow off the locks. In that moment, Gritchkin regained consciousness.

Even as Carter was squeezing the trigger, the Russian agent's fist was swinging up in a wide arc. His massive fist caught Carter in the right ear, causing all sorts of noise and pain in the American's head. The automatic pistol went off, but the bullets crashed harmlessly through the Plexiglas window above the Russian's head.

Time had run out for Nick Carter. The plane was at the gate, stopping as the end of the boarding tunnel moved smoothly out to meet it. And the second KGB guard was coming around, somewhere behind Carter's back. Still, he wouldn't let go. He was too close to the vital data that could hasten the end of life on much of the planet—and quite possibly all of it.

He crashed the pistol down on Gritchkin's head, then aimed for the locks again. Before he could fire this time, though, the guard behind him was up and swinging. Carter caught the hardness of revolver against the back of his head and felt his legs turning to rubber.

With the last ounce of his energy, he turned on the guard and fired a burst from the automatic pistol. The man doubled over, both hands on his stomach. His revolver went off, and the bullet plowed up a furrow in the plane's carpet.

''Hold it!'' a loud voice called from the forward part of the plane. ''Hold it right there!''

Carter peered through the tourist section and saw that an armed man in a green uniform, much like an air marshal on a U.S. flight, was aiming a .45-caliber pistol at him. He fired a burst and sent the marshal scooting for cover, then gave up the fight for the material in Gritchkin's briefcase.

He did the only thing available to him. He rushed to an emergency exit amidships and pulled the lever. The door popped open, and a huge yellow chute filled with air and flopped out onto the wing. Carter leaped through the opening and slid down the chute. From the wing, it was only a short drop to the tarmac.

And he was back to square one again, alive but without the briefcase or Gritchkin, and with his chances of ever getting either of them narrowed to the point of nonexistence.

To make matters worse, as he was racing across the tarmac toward a door to the baggage and maintenance section of the terminal, he heard a sound that put him into even greater depths of despair.

It was the *BAH-loop*, *BAH-loop*, *BAH-loop* of a Dutch police siren.

The captain of Flight 9 might not have been able to control Nick Carter while he was on the plane, but he had done the next best thing. He had radioed ahead and had the police waiting.

Carter turned to watch the police cruiser racing across the taxiways toward the big aircraft at the gate. He had perhaps ten seconds before it would arrive at his spot.

He turned again and ran smack into the arms of an enormous policeman who had just walked out of the baggage section.

EIGHT

Carter immediately pegged the big cop as an airport security guard, not a member of the Amsterdam police force. It didn't really matter. He hated to battle with police of any kind; his fight was with the forces that would tear down what many good men throughout history had built with blood, brains, courage, and even wisdom.

It was with a trace of regret, then, when he brought his knee sharply up into the guard's groin and watched the man fall retching to the ground. He stepped over the man and dashed inside the baggage section.

Common sense told him to get away from the airport as quickly as possible, because it would be swarming with police in a matter of minutes—and they'd have his description to a T. But he had to find out what Anatoly Gritchkin and the valuable briefcase would be doing while Aeroflot mechanics located and repaired the latest "mechanical difficulty" on Flight 9.

Carter located a maintenance shop, donned the white overalls that marked members of the maintenance crew, and left the shop on an electric cart designed to haul tools and workmen to any part of the enormous building. Schiphol was one of the most advanced and most sophisticated air terminals in the world.

He was becoming very familiar with the many concourses and corridors of the airport; he felt as if he'd taken up permanent residence there in the past twenty-four hours. He put the cart in high gear and moved up to the gate area where Flight 9 was parked and already discharging passengers. He eased the cart into a side corridor and watched the chattering passengers as they flocked past, still agitated, still frightened, and because of one more delay in a much-delayed flight, still angry.

Several policemen passed him and went down the loading tube to the plane, but the crew had not left the plane as yet. And there was no sign of Anatoly Gritchkin and his new guards. Minutes went by and still the crew and the KGB men did not emerge from the boarding tunnel. Carter resisted an impulse to check on what was happening in that plane. Too many Russians and now too many Dutch police and airport security people were looking for him, and they had a full and adequate description of what he looked like. He doubted that the white workman's uniform would be enough should anyone be serious about finding and stopping him.

Wearily, Nick Carter drove the electric maintenance cart to the main lobby, left it in plain sight of anyone who might be interested, and went to the nearest telephone booth.

"Tammi," he said, "come fetch me, for I am weary to heart and fain would lie doon."

"Oh, Nicholas, you're back!" Tammi cried into the telephone. "You're back and you're alive! Thank God!"

"And a few others," Carter said tiredly. "I blew it, Tammi. I blew the job and lost the man I was after. I need a place to lay my head for a minute or two, then I'll pick up his trail again. Will you come get me at the airport?"

"Thirty minutes, okay?"

"Twenty, if you can."

The captain of Flight 9 had indeed radioed ahead to notify the police of trouble aboard the aircraft and had given a description of the "Dutchman" who had caused it. Now, facing the wrath of Anatoly Gritchkin, the captain wished he had let the crazy Dutchman kill the chunky man with the black briefcase.

"You will tell the police that it was a mistake," Gritchkin said as the passengers filed off the plane. He, the captain, the copilot, and the flight engineer were locked in the cockpit. Police cars were all around the plane. The bodies of the steward and the KGB guard were secreted in the two rear lavatories. The blood in the cordoned-off rear area was being cleaned up by the remaining stewards and the other KGB guard.

"They will know I'm lying," the pilot said. "They saw the Dutchman themselves. He kicked a security guard in the groin and escaped inside the baggage section of the terminal. They're chasing him in there, I imagine."

"Who is to say that he came from Flight Nine?" Gritchkin demanded.

"There is the emergency exit with the yellow chute sticking out," the captain offered with a shrug.

"The stewards have taken care of that," Gritchkin said. "The police are not to come aboard this aircraft. And I will not get off until I am certain that this insane man has been caught. Meanwhile, I suggest that you have our glorious mechanics find out what is wrong with this plane. We must leave for Moscow within the next few hours. They are screaming for the data in this briefcase."

"Yes, Comrade Gritchkin," the captain said, holding

back a vituperative comment he was thinking about what the spy could do with the data in his damned briefcase. "I will keep the police away, and the stewards will prepare a place for you and your man to be comfortable."

"And the crew must remain aboard," Gritchkin said. "Until this plane leaves the ground again, no one but legitimate passengers are to leave or enter. Do I make myself clear?"

"Quite clear, Comrade Gritchkin."

"One exception," the agent said as he opened the door a crack to see if the passengers had left. "I will send for a replacement guard and he will be permitted aboard." He seemed to ponder a matter for a few seconds, then said, "One more exception. When I contact my people for a replacement guard, I will also arrange for someone to remove the bodies. I do not wish to spend the next few hours in a plane with people bleeding all over the place."

The passengers gone, Gritchkin stomped back into the tourist section and closed the heavy panels that separated it from first class. He gazed at the men working at the rear of the plane, cleaning up the remainder of the blood, then collapsed into a seat. His anger was spent on the captain, so his mind was clear to consider his options and to decide on how he could best complete his mission.

Anatoly Gritchkin was a latecomer to the overall scheme to steal American laser-satellite plans and sneak them back to Moscow. He knew nothing of the long years that special agents had worked on the U.S. Air Force pilot named John Parnell, or the years during which Parnell had infiltrated each key sensitive area of the U.S. program to control space with satellites armed with laser and particle beam weapons. Even if he had known, he couldn't have cared less.

Gritchkin was a professional in every sense of the word,

but he cared little for the intricacies of international espionage. He loved the suspense, the killing, the wild, riotous chases. In a gunfight, he could actually experience sexual, or at least sensual, thrills. He had thought that the man posing as a Dutch businessman was going to kill him in that crazy moment when the airplane was careening down the runway and the man was on top of him with the steward's automatic pistol.

In the moment that he thought he would die from a hail of bullets from that pistol, he had begun to become aroused. Now, slouched in the airplane seat near the scene of blood and death, he felt that sensation trying to return. Dammit, he wished he had a few more days and nights to spend in Europe—Western Europe, that is. What a swath he could cut through the nightclubs. He recalled the scenes between the enormous woman and the. . . .

"Enough," he said aloud, reminding himself that his mission was too important to be endangered again by his private wishes and follies. Stanislav, bless his old iron heart, had objected strenuously to that last fling in the West, and Stanislav, as far as Gritchkin knew, was now deader than a doornail. "Alas," Gritchkin mused out loud, "when you are dead, you are dead. No more women, no more sex, no more fun. Ah, fun. Ah, wine. Ah, women."

That the material in the briefcase was important and even vital to Soviet interests was taken for granted in the mind of the professional spy. God knew he'd played courier for a great number of briefcases filled with material that was important and vital to his country. The importance of a given set of data was decided by men bigger and more important than he, Gritchkin admitted—even men who were more intelligent.

And the Americans had made it very clear just how

important was the material in the black briefcase that he now held on his lap. They hadn't sent a whole force of men to retrieve it, but the man they had sent was obviously far more resourceful than even Gritchkin had expected. The man had anticipated his every move. Gritchkin had insisted to Stanislav that the man must have picked up their trail in West Germany and knew nothing of their true mission. He knew now that that was folly. The man had been onto him almost from the beginning.

And this bothered Anatoly Gritchkin. He'd been told that the Americans were onto the plan to get material back to Moscow but that everything was set to dupe them into thinking that it would leave from London. He'd be safe making his departure from Amsterdam. Some safety, he mused, as he glanced back at the bloody aisle again. And those bodies in the lavatories. God, how he wished they weren't there. The threat of death excited him; death itself left him with a feeling of disgust.

So he would contact his superior in Amsterdam and have another guard sent to the plane, and he'd have the bodies removed. But what about the man who had managed to get aboard this flight and almost ruin it all? Gritchkin entertained no foolish notions that such a man had been captured by the Dutch police. He had little respect for the Dutch, or their police.

What would the man do now that he'd been found out and now that he was on the run? Gritchkin tried to figure the man's options, using his own experience as a guide. Oh, he'd been cornered and almost caught a number of times during his long career. He'd escaped and he'd completed his missions and he'd always figured all the options, almost always choosing the right one. The phony Dutchman was also such a man, he decided, a veteran who knew instinctively what to do next.

Right now, this phony Dutchman who was an American agent of some kind was sitting in a room somewhere figuring his own options. He would be trying to decide what Anatoly Gritchkin would do next.

Would the Russian stay aboard the aircraft until it was repaired and then fly to Moscow? Or would Anatoly Gritchkin succumb to his carnal desires and leave the relative safety of the aircraft for the fleshpots of Belgium. Or, better yet, would the Soviet operative switch to another aircraft under cover of darkness (and it would be dark shortly) and fly away to glory in his homeland while the American still pondered what to do next?

There were many options open to him. Whatever he chose to do, he could be certain that the American would spend valuable time checking out all the options, while Gritchkin had only to pursue the one he chose.

Anatoly Gritchkin was, as the Americans would say, in the catbird seat.

He decided, as he waited for the men to clean up the mess in the rear of the plane and for the pilot to get rid of the police he had so foolishly called, that he liked that catbird seat and that he would like to sit in it just a while longer.

The big, important men in Moscow would just wait for their big, important mess of data that Anatoly Gritchkin carried in the black briefcase.

"Comrade Gritchkin?" the captain said tentatively as he approached the KGB agent who seemed asleep or lost in a pleasant reverie.

"Yes, what is it?" the spy demanded, opening his eyes to reality.

"I have sent the police away," the captain said. "And there is a message for you. You are to telephone this number immediately." He gave the spy a slip of paper on which a number was written. "If you like, I can arrange a telephone patch through the tower and—"

"Fool!" Gritchkin exclaimed. "You want every international espionage agency in the whole world to listen in? No, I'll have to go into the terminal and find a clean telephone. Have they caught the man who caused all the trouble on this aircraft?"

"He got away," the captain said woefully. "A blond woman was seen picking him up in front of the Aeroflot section."

"I don't doubt that," Gritchkin said, smacking his wide forehead with his hand. "I work with fools. It would not surprise me if you said that he drove away in the Aeroflot director's staff car. All right, I shall go to a telephone. When I return, perhaps your mechanics will have awakened and be aboard looking for the solution to this sea of problems that seems to have flooded over our great airline company."

Gritchkin dismissed the captain and went to fetch his remaining guard to accompany him into the terminal. He dreaded making the call. He recognized the number written on the paper the pilot had given him.

Somehow, the chief of his department had discovered the comedy of errors keeping Anatoly Gritchkin and his precious briefcase out of Russia, and was calling for an explanation.

Gritchkin had no explanation. None that his chief would consider legitimate, anyway.

In the city, in the swank Buitenveldert section, another man was wrestling with an identical problem—that of explaining to his chief why things had gone wrong.

"You mean you actually had your hands on that briefcase and you let it go? You didn't come away with it? I find that hard to believe, N3. Are you all right? Were you hurt during the flight?''

"No, sir," Carter told Hawk. "You really had to be there, sir. I mean, the briefcase was handcuffed to his wrist and there were men with guns and hysterical passengers and a plane that was about to stop. It was a tricky situation.''

"Somehow," Hawk muttered into the phone, "that doesn't make my day, N3. I'll accept that the circumstances weren't the best, but the material in that briefcase is—Christ, Nick, I can't believe that you had your hands on it and didn't take it out with you, even if you had to rip the man's hand off to get it.''

"I'm sorry, sir," Carter told his boss. He gave Tammi Krisler a long-suffering look and followed it with a wink. He wasn't enjoying the chewing out by Hawk, but he knew that the man's anger was short-lived. Hawk would come around in time.

"Do you want a backup?" Hawk asked. It was like a slap in the face to a man of Carter's ability and experience.

"If I feel the need for one," Carter said, suddenly serious, "I'll request a backup.''

"Do you know what your next step is going to be?" Hawk asked.

"Not yet. There are several options that—"

"I don't care about options," Hawk cut him short. "What are you going to do next? That's what I want to know. Are you going to drag Gritchkin off that plane and get his briefcase, or aren't you?"

"He may not even be on the plane now," Carter argued. "He may already have shifted to another one, although I've learned from the ticket agent that no other planes are ready to fly as yet. Even so, the man could switch planes and hole up until it's repaired.''

"All right," Hawk said. "Then why aren't you at the airport checking on things? By the way, where are you?"

"At a friend's house," Carter said.

"A woman?"

"Yes, sir."

"I thought so."

"Don't worry, sir," Carter said. "I won't be here long. I'll get back to the airport as soon as I can be certain the police don't have a trap set for me."

"Why would they have a trap set for you? I thought they were looking for a Dutch businessman."

"I'm leaving now, sir. Right away. No delay. Okay?"

"All right, N3," Hawk said the angry tone receding from his voice, "all right. I'll leave it in your capable hands. You know what we want and you know what you must do to get it. I don't suggest you go ripping off hands, but you might consider bringing in the whole man along with the briefcase."

"I've considered that," Carter replied. "It's just been tough to cut him out of the herd, so to speak. I'll work on that angle as soon as I determine just where he is and what he plans to do. Good-bye, sir."

He hung up before Hawk had a chance to add more fuel to his tirade. He took a deep breath, let it out, and gazed at Tammi with a slow grin.

"You heard the man, or at least my reaction to him," he told her while she was fixing drinks for them both. "I have to go—now, not later. When I learn what I need to know, perhaps there'll be time to come back. Will you wait for me?"

"Only forever," Tammi said, sighing. "Isn't there anything I can do to get you to put it off, even for a half hour or so?"

"Don't tempt me, hussy," he said, blowing her a kiss

as he turned to leave. "Keep the home fires burning. I shall return."

"Make it soon," Tammi said. "I go to work in four hours, you know."

"I forgot that some people work for a living," Carter said, grinning. "With luck, I'll be back in two hours. Good enough?"

"It will have to be," she said sadly.

"Oh, one thing," Carter said, his hand on the doorknob of the replaced front door. "My boss will have this number traced and know your address, just as the Russians did. There might be some unexpected callers in the next hour. They'll be harmless."

"Who will they be?" Tammi asked, her eyes widening with fear as she recalled the dawn assault by the five KGB men.

"Friends," Carter said with a cryptic smile. "They'll pretend to be meter readers and such, but they'll really be casing the place. Just be pleasant, and they'll retreat to a safe distance and watch. I told my boss I didn't need a backup, but sometimes he doesn't listen to me and does what he thinks is best. The men will be here to protect both of us."

With that, Carter went out to the red Volvo in the driveway. He had asked for the green one, but someone else had rented it.

At Schiphol Airport, with all traces of the obnoxious Dutch businessman gone, Nick Carter left the Volvo in the parking lot and walked casually past the Aeroflot counter. He didn't recognize the ticket agent, then remembered the time. It was a different shift.

Carter stopped to study the television monitor that told of arriving and departing Aeroflot flights. All flights showed delays. Just to make certain, the man from AXE went to the counter.

"My wife and I are thinking of going to Warsaw," he told the agent. "Can you tell me when the next flight will leave?"

"It shouldn't be very long, sir," the agent said. "Though most of our long-distance flights have been canceled due to unexpected circumstances, we expect to have one aircraft flight-ready in two hours."

Carter glanced at the clock behind the counter. It was five minutes before five. "Will the flight leave at seven?" he asked.

"Oh, no, sir," the agent said. "The plane should be ready by then, but we will have to call all the passengers who are waiting before setting a time. I would think that Flight Nine could leave by ten tonight. Would you like me to write tickets for you and your wife?"

"Not just yet," Carter said. "I told her I would check. She might want to wait until tomorrow. What are the chances for a flight to Warsaw tomorrow?"

"Very good," the agent said. "We will have all our aircraft operational by then. I'll be happy to make out your tickets if you wish. There will be plenty of available seats."

Carter left, toying with the idea of playing mechanic again, of sabotaging all of Aeroflot's big planes. But it was an unnecessary risk. All he needed to do was stop one plane, or at least be on it.

As he was nearing the checkpoint for the west concourse where Flight 9 had arrived earlier from its aborted Warsaw flight, Carter was surprised to see the aircraft still sitting at the gate, the portable loading tunnel still in place. He had expected the Russians to take the plane into the hangar to have it repaired.

Carter stood at the window and watched as mechanics swarmed around the plane, checking its exterior, with special attention to the rudder and elevator section. He could see through the windows of the darkened plane, see the white coveralls of mechanics moving back and forth in there. *Check the starboard lavatory,* he said to himself. *Take off the panel to the control box and you'll see where I've shaved a couple of wires down to a nub. You could have this plane ready in five minutes if you knew where to look.*

But the thorough Russian mechanics would check the plane from one end to the other before they'd stoop to the obvious. Perhaps it was that way with all mechanics.

As he stood by the window and watched the mechanics at work, or playing at work, he wondered if Anatoly Gritchkin was also inside that plane with the briefcase. Perhaps. Perhaps not. In any event, he stood no chance of getting aboard that plane and out again, with or without the briefcase, with or without his skin.

He was about to move on, to get closer to the gate, when he heard a familiar voice speaking Russian. He cocked his head without fully turning.

Anatoly Gritchkin and two men were walking toward the checkpoint. Carter recognized one of the men as the KGB guard he had hit behind the ear while the plane was making its violent landing. The other was new to him, perhaps a recruit from that gang of guards on the thirtieth floor of the Nederlands Hilton.

"The fools won't have the plane ready for six or seven hours," Gritchkin was saying in Russian to his guards. He still had the briefcase clutched to his bosom, Carter noted. Gritchkin went on: "They say two hours, but I know from experience how they exaggerate. Have the limousine and three other guards at the main entrance in a half hour. We can be in Antwerp in less than an hour after that. After dinner, I guarantee you that you will see a show that you'll never forget. And then . . ."

The men passed out of earshot. Carter could hardly believe his good luck.

The spy planned to stick it out with the ups and downs of Flight 9. Furthermore, he planned to have another final fling at the infamous Chez Carlo and its bizarre act in Antwerp.

With a grin, Nick Carter turned from the checkpoint and walked breezily out to the parking lot and the red Volvo.

Tammi had said she wanted him for a half hour and, by God, she would have him for a half hour.

NINE

"Nicholas, you're crazy," Tammi said as they lay side by side in her satin-sheeted bed in the pink bedroom. Soft music played from speakers in each corner of the room. Carter had told her about his narrow escape on Flight 9 and how he would follow Gritchkin on another junket to Antwerp and perhaps beyond.

"I've known that for years," Carter replied, tracing one of her nipples with the tip of his forefinger. He was lying on his side, facing her. They had not made love yet. Tammi liked the suspense to build before he made love to her, and Carter was a master of suspense—sexual and otherwise.

"But don't you see what's happening?" Tammi pleaded. "They're laying a trap for you." She quivered under the attention he was paying to that small, pink, erect nipple. Carter bent down and kissed the downy hairs around her deep navel. "They'll catch you on the highway someplace and the last thing anyone sees of you will be a ball of flame."

"Possibly," he said, moving his lips downward while his hand clasped the nipple and the swell of breast around it. Tammi gasped and began kissing his wide, naked shoulders. "I might even say it's a probability instead of a mere possibility. What else would you have me do?"

"Stay here with me," she said.

"A much more pleasant but impossible alternative," he said, chuckling as his lips brushed the softness of her belly. "The last time I slept here, we both nearly got blown away."

"Oh, Nicholas," Tammi gasped, "I don't want anything to happen to you. I don't—oh, Nick, I don't know what you're doing down there, but don't stop. Please, don't stop . . ."

Carter had no intentions of stopping. He had found the most sensitive part of her, and his tongue was doing its best to drive her just as crazy as she claimed him to be. He felt her shift beneath him and felt her warm hands slip down between them, caressing his thighs.

He had to admit that Tammi had a point about the trap. He had considered it a prime possibility from the beginning. It was no accident, he felt, that Gritchkin chose that moment in time as he passed by Carter at the airport to tell his KGB guards of his plans to return to Antwerp. But if the spy had known that it was Carter standing there beside the window, why wouldn't he have just blown him away, ending the threat to his plans forever?

The answer was simple yet complex. If the spy had known that the man by the window was Carter—or the agent who had been aboard the Aeroflot plane posing as a Dutch businessman—he would not have acted for fear that a dozen like him lurked in the shadows. Only Carter—and Hawk, of course—knew that he was working virtually alone on this case. They had decided in Hawk's office in the Amalgamated Press and Wire Services Building, AXE's front organization on Dupont Circle in Washington, that the job called for one man, that a brace of agents—even if they were available—would tend to clutter up the scene.

It had been Hawk's clever thinking that had alerted Carter to the possibility that Colonel John Parnell, the U.S. Air Force officer who'd sold out, might not be the one to take the laser-satellite data out of Europe. Carter hadn't been surprised when Parnell told him of Gritchkin, nor had he been shocked when the Russians wasted Parnell and the lovely Andrea Boritsky. That was SOP for the KGB.

He was surprised, however, that the KGB kept a man like Gritchkin on such an important mission. Ordinarily, he knew, the Soviets would have changed their plans radically at the first sign of trouble, especially on a matter of such vital strategic importance as the material contained in the black briefcase handcuffed to Gritchkin's wrist.

Gritchkin was good, Carter knew, but his weakness was too common and too fatal in this business. Sooner or later, the Russian's penchant for the bizarre and eerie in matters of sex would lead him and his mission to failure and disaster.

But that wasn't Carter's problem. His problem was in deciding whether Gritchkin deliberately told of his planned second trip to Antwerp to trap Carter into following, or whether the whole thing was coincidental. No matter what he decided, the opposite could be true, so he would naturally be on his guard when he followed Gritchkin and his KGB companions to Antwerp.

"Nicholas, have you gone to sleep on me?" Tammi's voice floated to him on a cloud of sexual ardor. The dark-haired man had slackened in his attentions to the blond woman's needs—needs that he himself had aroused and set aflame.

''Not nearly,'' he said, sending a stab of joy deep within the woman's body. Her lips were on him now, and he moved his hips slowly on the bed, savoring the soft wetness of her.

She was panting now from the fruits of his labors below. She worked more diligently at what she was doing to him and had the satisfaction of feeling him become even more excited.

Carter kissed his way slowly up her body, briefly buried his handsome, chiseled face between her wondrous breasts, and found her lips with his. She guided him to her and they joined, and without further words, they moved smoothly together until the music in the room no longer came only from the stereo speakers.

Panting, emotionally and physically spent for the moment, the man known in only one tight circle as a Killmaster held on to his lady and slid with her into the tender aftermath of violent lovemaking. Tammi kept kissing him lightly on his neck, just below his ear. He caressed her slender white throat. A great drowsiness was about to overcome them both.

Carter forced himself to stay awake, but he spoke soothingly to the woman and kept caressing her throat. Soon she was sound asleep. He slipped from her embrace, and wondering if he'd ever return to it, dressed and left the house.

The man on the roof of the house across the street from Tammi Krisler's huge domain was Aleksi Veronovitch. He was one of twenty-six men brought in specially to protect the man named Anatoly Gritchkin while the man was at the Nederlands Hilton. An hour before Boris Stanislav went out, never to return, Stanislav had given Veronovitch an address and had said that if he did not come back, the low-level KGB guard was to watch the house at that address from a safe distance.

If he saw a man come and go often, Stanislav said, Veronovitch was to consider the man the American agent who had apparently stumbled onto the scheme to sneak Gritchkin and some valuable data out of the country. When Veronovitch thought the time was right, he was to kill the American. Veronovitch was by nature and specialty an assassin, a skilled sharpshooter who would rather shoot a man than an inanimate target.

Early this morning, Aleksi Veronovitch had detached himself from the guard contingent at the hotel and had entered the house across from the place that Stanislav designated. He had killed the man and woman living there, and had hidden their bodies in the basement. Then he had taken up his position on the roof, from where he had a clear view of the house across the street.

With a special Weatherby Mark V rifle provided by a Dutch contact with lines to American weapons suppliers, Veronovitch knew that he would not miss, even if he had to shoot through a window of the house across the street. In fact, he had watched through the keen Bausch & Lomb scope a most delightful scene. He had watched the American agent making love to a blond woman in an upstairs bedroom of that house.

At one point, Veronovitch had his finger on the trigger and the back of the dark-haired man in the cross hairs of the scope. He had squeezed gently, itching to kill the man now. But he wanted the man out on the street where he could see him double over in pain and perhaps even shout from the agony of the copper-sheathed missile that Veronovitch would send down to tear at his vitals.

Now the man was coming out of the house and was walking toward the red Volvo in which he had arrived not

more than a half hour ago. Aleksi Veronovitch tracked the
man in the cross hairs, and when the man was at the door
of the Volvo, Veronovitch's finger tightened on the trigger.

Unknown to Veronovitch, he had been under surveillance since shortly after his arrival at the house in the
Buitenveldert section of Amsterdam. A man sent there by
Hawk to make certain that no harm came to an agent
designated as N3, had been sitting in a car several yards
down the street when Aleksi Veronovitch arrived in his
tiny Volkswagen. The man had immediately pegged Veronovitch as low-level KGB and had watched his every
movement. Even so, the man sent by the chief of AXE had
not seen what happened inside the house when Veronovitch killed the couple living there. The agent had
stumbled onto the bodies later and had worked up a
tremendous hatred for the man who had killed those innocent people.

The unknown (unknown to Carter, that is) AXE operative had also watched the man designated as N3 come and
go to the house across the street on a previous occasion
and had seen him return just over a half hour ago. He had
not watched the house. He had watched Veronovitch from
behind a chimney as the Russian waited with a big Weatherby Mark V.

The AXE agent had his own weapon, a Walther PPG
equipped with a silencer, trained on the Russian. He had
seen the man's finger work the trigger of the Weatherby
on a number of occasions but had known instinctively that
the killer wasn't serious about firing.

He knew with those same instincts that Aleksi Veronovitch was now preparing to pull the trigger and, no
doubt, kill the man designated as N3.

There was only a small popping sound as the AXE
guardian fired his Walther.

There was the smacking sound of struck flesh. There was a soft gasp and a low moan as the hunk of hot lead from the pistol crunched through Aleksi Veronovitch's spine, severing it, and sending out a fireburst of blood, flesh, and bone.

Nick Carter, who had paused with his hand on the door handle of the red Volvo, had a keen sense of danger for just a moment. His sharp eyes scanned the yard of Tammi Krisler's house and settled on the roof of the innocent-looking house across the wide street.

Something was amiss over there. He felt eyes on him. He felt that more than eyes were trained on him. For an instant, he steeled his body for some kind of shock, perhaps even excruciating pain or an abysmal blackness.

The instant passed and the sense of danger dissipated. Without knowing why, Carter knew that the danger was over. He opened the door, got into the Volvo, and fired up its smooth but powerful engine.

Anatoly Gritchkin felt a sense of almost childlike rebellion as the black limousine moved southward on E-10 out of Amsterdam. He was glad now that he had called his section chief a second time. The bawling out had been repeated, but the logic of Gritchkin's next move was now officially sanctioned.

He was getting what he wanted, and he would also satisfy his chief and assure himself of that hero's welcome in certain circles in Moscow.

When Gritchkin had dialed the number written on the piece of paper given him by the captain of once-again-disabled Flight 9, he had done so with trembling, sweating fingers. The familiar voice of his chief had droned and then cracked on the line, causing an enormous cocktail of fears fizz in Gritchkin's intestines.

"You should have blown the man away, as the

Americans say,'' his chief reiterated. ''You had the firepower in that black limousine you insist on riding around in. As soon as the American revealed that he was following you, you should have given yourself the benefit of the doubt, decided that he was onto your plan, and blown him away. Why didn't you? No, don't answer that, Anatoly. I know why. We all know why. You were too busy chasing your own pleasure to disturb your fun with a killing. You thought it was over when the man was arrested by the Dutch police. Come, comrade, stop playing the fool. If we can buy the police, so can the Americans. You knew he would be free in a matter of minutes and would come after you. And now you insist on taking Flight Nine out of Amsterdam when we could arrange to have you driven to another European airport where you can wait for an Aeroflot flight. I should like to hear your rationale for remaining in Amsterdam. Well, comrade, has the cat got your tongue?''

Gritchkin had argued well. If the borders were being watched, he said, other airports would certainly be under surveillance. Plus, he had seen the American spy in the concourse near the checkpoint to the section from where the Aeroflot plane would depart. He told of how he had made sure the man overheard him say that he and a few men would drive that evening to Antwerp for dinner.

''The American will certainly follow,'' Gritchkin had argued. ''When he does, we will do what you suggest we should have done when we discovered him on our trail. You are right there, comrade. It was a mistake on my part not to have him eliminated then. I apologize with utmost humility. But I was so certain that the man who caused all the trouble in London would never show up in Amsterdam that I considered the man to be a local agent, merely curious as to why a carload of Russian diplomats were in his country. Our car does have diplomatic license plates, you know.''

"I know. The ambassador has complained many times about the fact that you are keeping one of his precious automobiles occupied.''

"After tonight,'' Gritchkin said, "the ambassador may have his car back and we will have a dead American agent alongside the Antwerp highway. You can depend on it.''

"We have depended on having you and the material on the U.S. White Horse project in our hands for two days now,'' the chief reminded Gritchkin.

"This time,'' Gritchkin argued, "even if he survives our trap on the highway, there is no way he can get aboard the flight. The captain of the flight does not know it yet, but I do not intend for Flight Nine to carry regular passengers when it is ready to depart. There will be myself and a few hand-picked comrades from our section, all well armed and all with a description of the man trying to stop me. I have pieced together a description from several people who have seen him, both when he was following us in Belgium, West Germany, and the Netherlands, and when he posed as a Dutch businessman. He might wear different clothes and a mustache and affect a different speech, but he cannot conceal his bearing and stature. There is something decidedly special about this man and I saw it in the man standing alongside the concourse window.''

Gritchkin also told of how he'd sent one of his agents to follow the man and had seen him get into a red Volvo and drive to the exclusive Buitenveldert section. It was the same house, he said, where they had discovered that Boris Stanislav and four of their best men were murdered by a mysterious assailant. The KGB man, pretending to be a Dutch police detective, had talked to neighbors and received a description of a man who had been seen leaving the vicinity in a green Volvo, then in a red Volvo.

"It is the same man," Gritchkin concluded.

"I see. And your plan is to repeat a part of last night's performance and kill the man when he follows?"

"Yes, comrade. That is precisely my plan."

There was a pause, and Gritchkin knew that his chief was trying to decide whether the spy had a real case here or was just looking for another opportunity to spend state money for a frivolous night in a club known for its highly unusual entertainment. The chief could be manipulated to a certain degree, but he was no dummy, Gritchkin knew.

"There remains a puzzle," the chief said. "I received a call a few minutes ago from a man named Aleksi Veronovitch. He worked for Stanislav. He said he was in a house across the street from this place where the American goes to be with the blond Dutchwoman, the nightclub singer, and he said that the American agent Stanislav suspected was trailing you was in the house having an affair with the woman. He also said that he had instructions to kill the man when he emerged. He is to call me back within a few minutes to give me results. If he kills the American, there will be no reason for you to endanger the mission further by going to Antwerp. There will be no need to set a trap. I suggest you call me back in ten minutes."

And Anatoly Gritchkin had done so, praying that this Aleksi Veronovitch would not kill the American. He wanted that pleasure, along with a few other pleasures he had in mind and for which a huge appetite remained.

"Go to Antwerp," the chief had said tersely, without explanation. "Do what must be done. As soon as the aircraft has been repaired, carry out your mission as outlined. Meanwhile, I shall contact the airline and make certain you have no problems regarding the refusal to take passengers. You and your men will be alone on the plane with the crew.''

Now, riding in the plush back seat of the limousine and sipping a glass of excellent Dutch brandy, Anatoly Gritchkin was a happy man indeed. There was only one small worry. They had driven twelve miles from Amsterdam and there was no sign of the American agent in the red Volvo. There was no sign of anyone following.

Well, he thought, recalling his pleasure at Chez Carlo and the fact that he would repeat it after dinner, *there is time. He will follow and we will eliminate him.*

After leaving Tammi Krisler's house, Nick Carter had driven only a few miles south of the city and had pulled off onto a side street to wait. Since he knew that Gritchkin was laying a trap for him, he also knew that the man would use the same route as the night before. But there was always the possibility that Gritchkin had lured him away from the city so that he and his playmates could fly off to Moscow undetected. Carter wanted to remain fairly close to the city, and certainly close to the airport, in case the black limo didn't show.

After a ten-minute wait, he began to be concerned. He decided that he would give Gritchkin another ten minutes and then strike out for the airport. If worst came to worst, Carter decided, he'd talk Hawk into a truly radical move.

If Gritchkin pulled another trick out of his bag and really did take off for Moscow while Carter was waiting for him on the road to Antwerp, he'd ask that the plane be shot down before it left Western air space. If the shooting down of a Korean Airlines commercial aircraft by the Soviets hadn't sparked a world war, the destruction of an Aeroflot commerical flight was an acceptable risk.

It would be a terrible thing to have happen, Carter

knew, just as the shooting down of the Korean plane had been terrible. But the destruction caused by the one-sided war the Soviets planned if they gained a significant edge in what scientists and militarists already were calling ''the *Star Wars* syndrome'' was simply too terrible to contemplate.

Nick Carter had little doubt that, in an extreme situation, Hawk would approve such an action as the shooting down of a Soviet commercial aircraft.

But Carter wasn't disappointed in his wait for Gritchkin. Long before his ten-minute limit had been reached, the limousine cruised past on the main highway, and Carter moved out slowly. Since he knew where the limousine was going, and was now satisfied that Gritchkin hadn't lied, he stayed back several miles, most of the time not even in sight of the limousine.

He dreaded the distasteful nightclub act he'd probably have to witness while waiting for Gritchkin's men to make their move. Then again, perhaps the trap was to be sprung on the way to Antwerp. Either way, Carter had made up his mind not to give the KGB agent and his gunmen a crack at him until they were on the way back.

By that time, Carter reasoned, the men would be logy from wine and far less alert than usual. If he hoped to carry out his own plan of isolating Gritchkin from his men and of somehow separating the spy from that briefcase—even if it meant, as Hawk suggested, ripping the man's hand off—he wanted every possible advantage to be on his side.

Carter drove slowly along E-10 and did not see the small blue Renault that kept a considerable distance behind him.

As the lights of Antwerp loomed on the southern horizon, Carter did not see the headlights of the Renault close the gap between the two cars. He was watching ahead, fearful of once again coming too close to his quarry and being discovered, as he had near Nijmegen.

But the Renault was moving up swiftly, its windows down, and two men in the passenger seat and rear seat were readying AK-47 assault rifles.

TEN

Just north of Merksem in the northern suburbs of Antwerp there is a long bridge that crosses a small river and a deep ravine. At the bridge's approach, the highway makes a radical turn to the left. On the left side of the highway is a high cliff, reaching up to lovely homes. On the right, there is a ravine, filled with boulders and scrub pines and twisted but thick trees.

The curve is known in English parlance as "dead man's curve."

And even though Nick Carter approached the curve with utmost caution, considering it a prime area for an ambush, he paid small heed to the tiny Renault that was moving up into his blind spot and whirring like an overworked sewing machine.

Carter was looking for another limousine, or any powerful car filled with sharpshooters.

The little Renault, barely large enough to accommodate the driver and the two gunmen, would have appeared no more dangerous, even if Carter had seen it, than one of the thousands of motor scooters that populated the highways and city streets of the Netherlands and Belgium.

Carter was still pondering the distance between his own car and the black limousine when the Renault drew

110

alongside. In his peripheral vision, he caught sight of the
men at the windows. He saw the jutting barrels of the
Russian assault rifles.

By the time he had snapped his head around and was
reaching for Wilhelmina, the automatic rifles were already at work.

A thundering crash of copper-sheathed bullets riddled
the red Volvo. Glass shattered, metal *pinged*. The two
left-side tires blew simultaneously, and Carter saw that
the gunman in the rear seat had been concentrating on
those tires. The gunman beside the driver was swinging
his weapon back and forth alongside the Volvo, seemingly trying to cut off the top of the car along with Carter's
head.

Somewhere in the midst of all that roar and clatter, the
Killmaster ducked. In fact he fell sideways in the seat,
abandoning the steering wheel to the fates.

The bullets kept pouring from the AK-47 rifles.

Carter felt the right-side tires on the shoulder of the
road, then heard the screech of metal as the car began to
scrape alongside the steel guardrail. There was a crunch-
ing thump, and Carter knew that the car's bumper had
struck one of the guardrail's stanchions.

The red Volvo spun violently to the left, and Carter
gripped the seat cushion, preparing himself for another
jolt. He was certain that the car had shot out into the
highway again and would momentarily be soundly
whacked by a truck or another speeding car.

Instead, the car plunged back into the guardrail. Carter
heard another screech of metal on metal, then felt the
Volvo break free as it plunged outward over the ravine.

"Jesus, I've bought the farm," he muttered aloud.

He raised his head just in time to see the little Renault
pull to a stop several yards beyond where the Volvo had

plunged through the guardrail. He saw the jagged ends of the rail silhouetted against the cliff across the road and the lights of lovely mansions far above that. He spun his head to look through the shattered windshield.

The Volvo had nosed over and was heading for a patch of twisted trees and boulders. Carter had just enough time to berate himself for falling for such an obvious trick.

Gritchkin and his comrades were far too smart to have used the limousine as a part of the trap, too smart to have used a follow-up limo. They had known that Carter wouldn't initiate a close pursuit, that he would lay back and take his time following them to Chez Carlo in Antwerp.

It was a simple matter, then, to have their own men lay back also, in a small, nondescript car, and to spring the trap in the most obvious place—at a time when Carter would be looking for some really heavy action.

The use of the single Renault and two men with assault rifles wasn't necessarily a stroke of genius, but it had fooled Carter; it had worked.

Carter had less than two seconds to berate himself before the Volvo slammed into the trunk of a twisted linden tree. The car seemed about to wrap itself around the tree, when its momentum sent it plummeting toward the dark ground, shearing off branches as it went.

Even though the branches slowed the plunging car, the Volvo still struck the boulders with a teeth-jarring thud. Carter's head struck the steering wheel, broke the wheel into four pieces, then slammed back against the headrest. A wave of dizziness and nausea swept over him. He was losing consciousness, and with the last of his energy, he turned to look up the hill.

There, standing between the jagged edges of the broken guardrail, were the three men who had been in the Renault. Another car had stopped several hundred yards up the highway, but Carter thought little of it. The three men directly above were his greatest concern. As soon as they were certain that the Volvo wouldn't blow up from spilled gasoline, they would come down to check.

If they found Nick Carter alive, they'd put out his lights once and for all. It was, Carter mused with his last conscious thought, a no-win situation.

The man designated as Nick Carter's temporary guardian—and who had already killed to save the Killmaster's life—stood in darkness and watched the three men farther along the highway. The three men were at a gap in the guardrail, at the place where Carter's red Volvo had crashed through.

The AXE ''guardian'' knew precisely why the men with the AK-47 assault rifles hesitated to go down into the ravine. The gasoline tank of the Volvo could blow at any second.

The man who had killed Aleksi Veronovitch on the roof across the street from Tammi Krisler's house had no such qualms. The tank might indeed explode. Then again it might not. Either way, his instructions were clear: if there was a chance that Nick Carter was alive, all risk must be taken to preserve that life.

The man pocketed his Walther PPG and started down the steep cliff with a lack of caution that bordered on the reckless.

Even as he plunged down into the darkness, the man kept one eye on the three men above. If they decided to go down to check on whether their prey had survived the incredible plunge into the ravine, they would wind up killing two AXE agents instead of one. The Walther, even in the hands of Carter's unknown guardian, was no match for Russian assault weapons in the hands of the KGB agents.

Even so, the man did not hesitate in his mad plunge to the bottom of the ravine. When he was within ten yards of the wreck that had once been a shiny and powerful red Volvo, the man decided that no life could exist in that mass of twisted, tortured steel. Still, he had to make certain, just as the three killers above would eventually have to make certain.

The "guardian" reached the wreck and peered inside, wishing he dared use the tiny flashlight in his pocket. He could see the outline of the unconscious Nick Carter slumped over the broken steering wheel. He could make out, from reflected light from passing cars above, a wide swath of glistening blood down the forehead of the man from AXE. He reached in to press his fingers on Carter's carotid artery, checking for a pulse.

There was a pulse, very faint. The "guardian" grasped Carter beneath the armpits and gave a gentle tug. His eyes probed the darkness below, fearful that the Killmaster was pinned in the wreckage. He saw nothing there and had a moment's fear that perhaps Carter's legs had been severed or crushed.

The legs were apparently intact, he decided, because he couldn't move Carter's heavy body. N3 was not a huge man, but his six-foot frame was well-muscled from years of rigorous activity. He was, the man tugging at him decided, made of flesh and bone that were closely akin to granite.

After one hefty tug, the man felt Carter's body shift from the bucket seat. At the same time, a groan escaped Carter's blood-covered lips.

"Good signs," the "guardian" muttered under his breath. And then came the bad signs.

Just as the man was dragging Carter's still unconscious body from the wreckage, he smelled gasoline and heard it trickling from the ruptured tank. One miscue, one scraping of metal to cause a spark, and the long-awaited fireball would be at hand.

A second bad sign came from above.

The three would-be killers, two of them with automatic rifles, were coming down into the ravine.

Nick Carter had come to slightly when he felt something pulling at his shoulders. He had felt an excruciating pounding in his head and knew that he had a wound up there someplace. He tasted his own salty blood on his lips. But he couldn't bring himself to full awareness, no matter how much he tried.

Carter felt the continued tugging at his shoulders and knew that someone had him under the arms and was dragging him from the wrecked car. He tried to open his eyes, but he couldn't. He drifted in and out of consciousness, at one time feeling jagged pieces of metal, glass, and rough ground digging into his buttocks and back as he was dragged along, at another time feeling nothing and knowing nothing.

Once, Carter was certain, he heard people clambering down the side of the ravine. More people coming to his rescue? *They'd better stay clear of that damned car*, he thought in a moment of lucidity. From the smell of the gasoline, it might blow at any moment. And then he lapsed again into unconsciousness and couldn't have cared less.

He awoke to a sharp slapping on his already bruised and swollen cheeks. A man he had never seen before had Carter's head cradled in his lap. Carter's back and legs still lay against jagged rocks, and his head still pounded

like a jackhammer. Carter glanced around him and saw
that the man had dragged him fifty yards from the wrecked
car, almost to the narrow river.

He also saw that three men, two of them with AK-47s,
were coming down the steep incline and were within a few
yards of the wrecked Volvo.

"Come out of it, N3," the man said to Carter as he
continued slapping the sore cheeks. "I need the extra
firepower of your famous Luger. Come on, wake up!
There's no time to waste!"

Carter wondered who the man was and how he knew
about the code designate N3 and the Luger Carter called
Wilhelmina. He didn't wonder for long. The key words
and thoughts struck his now alert brain.

Three men were near the wreck, about to discover that
Carter was no longer inside it—that he was, instead, alive
and well somewhere nearby in the dark ravine. Two of
those men had automatic rifles and the ability to use them
with a high degree of expertise.

Still half in a daze, Carter raised to a sitting position.
The painful pounding in his head increased by multiples of
ten. He wiped blood from around his eyes and, with a
bloody hand, snaked Wilhelmina from its snug holster.

"Forget the extra firepower," he said to his unknown
benefactor. "I see something that will silence those
damned Russian choppers for good."

The "guardian" was about to protest. His Walther was
already aimed at one of the men carrying an AK-47. And
then he saw what Carter had seen and at what he was
aiming his Luger.

Gasoline was trickling from the tank down over the
twisted chassis of the wrecked Volvo. Each time a car
passed on the highway above, diffused light from its
beams made the gasoline glisten the way the blood on
Carter's forehead had glistened. A well-aimed bullet

would touch off the spilling gasoline.

But the ensuing blast might also take out Carter and the man who had rescued him.

"We're too close," the rescuer said. "Let's move back and then—"

"To hell with that," Carter rasped. "They've just learned that the car's empty. Hit the dirt, friend, and hit it hard!"

Wilhelmina boomed in the still night. The sound of that heavy charge of gunpowder in the Luger's breech crashed into the side of the ravine and ricocheted back and forth.

Carter poured three more rounds into the wreck, making certain that the 9mm slugs bounced off gasoline-soaked hunks of metal, then flopped to the ground just as an immense fireball began to rise around the wreck.

In the instant before his face hit the harsh gravel, he saw the three Russians, saw the rifles being raised. The figures were back-lighted by the flames for only that instant, but the image was seared on Carter's memory forever.

He didn't have to see what happened next. He felt the concussion of the thunderous blast as the gasoline tank exploded. A fraction of a second later, he felt the heat as the fireball rolled out and over him and his rescuer.

The three Russians, Carter knew, had either been incinerated or blown to bits in that crashing moment.

Carter gave a slow ten-count before he dared raise his head to see what his shooting had wrought. The fireball had dissipated, but flames still licked around the wrecked car and in a perimeter of perhaps a dozen yards. Flames even licked up the gnarled tree that had literally saved Carter from being crushed to death by the impact of landing at the bottom of the ravine.

Then Carter felt heat nearby. He turned toward the man who had saved his life.

And he felt ill.

His unknown benefactor hadn't followed Carter's advice. He hadn't hit the dirt. He had apparently been watching when Carter fired those four rounds from Wilhelmina, making certain that the bullets did the job N3 had intended for them to do.

He had caught the concussion and the fireball full in the face. Now that face was a mass of charred flesh, covered by hands that were equally blackened by heat and flame.

Even now, as the man lay on his back, dead, flames licked at his clothing.

"Damn!" Carter swore. "Dammit to hell!"

Choking back an emotional upheaval, Nick Carter patted out the flames. He looked back toward the wreck, checking just in case one of the three Russians had survived. None had. He saw remnants of their bodies hanging from the twisted trees. Flames licked at the remnants, but Carter felt no compulsion to pat out those flames.

With difficulty, Carter searched the pockets of the man who had saved his life.

The man's name, according to his passport, was Jonathan Wheeler. The name meant nothing to Carter. He examined the Walther PPG but found no clues to the man's true identity there. On impulse, he raised the man's sleeve, and there was the tattoo that identified the dead man as an agent of AXE, the world's smallest, most secret, and most deadly organization ever devised to fight against those who would destroy all that Nick Carter and men like him held sacred.

In a moment of insight, Carter recalled his feeling earlier, when he had left Tammi Krisler's house. He had felt troubled, endangered. The feeling had built to an almost unbearable climax, then had dissipated instantly. The danger had seemed to emanate from the house across the street.

Carter guessed that the man lying before him with the charred face and hands had been at that house earlier. He was convinced that, when he checked, he would find evidence of the man's presence there.

Right now, though, there were other problems. As much as his soul cried out for a few moments of silent meditation and respect for this fine young man who had died for him, he knew that he had to move swiftly.

The fireball and explosion had attracted motorists. Several people were standing alongside the highway at the broken guardrail. None showed signs of wanting to venture down into the ravine, but Carter could hear police and emergency vehicle sirens far in the distance. Someone had alerted the authorities.

Soon the ravine would be bustling with activity.

There was the problem of getting away from this scene of destruction without being delayed by police and their interminable questions.

And there was a potential problem back at Tammi's house. If danger had existed there earlier, perhaps this observant agent had eliminated it, but perhaps he only thought he had. Tammi could be in great danger.

Once again, Carter had underestimated Anatoly Gritchkin.

It was, he decided, the last time that would happen.

ELEVEN

As Nick Carter half walked, half stumbled up the narrow river, he tried in his foggy mind to figure out what had happened here and to map out his next moves.

The AXE agent named Jonathan Wheeler apparently had been assigned by Hawk to cover Carter's moves. The Russians had tracked Carter once to Tammi Krisler's house and had apparently staked it out. Wheeler, in turn, had staked out the stakeout, then had somehow followed Carter and the Russians on this second junket to Antwerp.

Even though his head hurt like hell and his heart ached for the cruel death that had come to his fellow AXE agent and rescuer, he felt a smile begin inside as he thought of how Anatoly Gritchkin had been followed by Carter, who had been followed by the gunmen in the Renault, who had been followed by Jonathan Wheeler.

A whole caravan of spies and counterspies roaming over the lovely Dutch and Belgian countryside, plotting death, destruction, and deceit.

But there remained even more complex situations to ponder.

Carter recalled seeing a car pull up behind the Renault, at a safe distance behind, and turn off its headlights. He had no doubt now that Jonathan Wheeler had arrived in that car and that the car was still where Wheeler had left it.

The keys had to be inside because they hadn't been in Wheeler's pockets when Carter had searched.

And, Carter worried, when Wheeler left his stakeout at Tammi Krisler's house, perhaps the Russians knew of his departure and still had plans for Tammi. He had to get to her, to determine if she were safe and then to guarantee her continued safety.

Soon, he guessed, word would reach Anatoly Gritchkin at Chez Carlo, if that was indeed where the spy had gone, that his three men had killed the American spy but had died in the attempt. Gritchkin wouldn't know immediately which spy had been killed—the one following him or the one who had staked out Tammi Krisler's house. It didn't matter. The Russian would know that one American lived and he would be wary, on guard.

Meanwhile, if Carter could only get that goddamned pounding to stop in his head. . . .

He left the river and started climbing well beyond where Wheeler had parked his car at the top of the ravine. Red lights above were whirling and blinking. Men with stretchers were starting the perilous climb down.

Carter touched his head gingerly, and found a mass of wet, drying, and dried blood matted in his hair. The pain came from a point in the center of his forehead, beginning at the hairline and extending back to his crown. He'd taken a hell of a bang there and was amazed that he was conscious, much less climbing a steep bank toward the highway.

When Carter reached the guardrail, he crouched behind it while he surveyed the scene farther down the road. Four police cars and two ambulances were there. Traffic had been halted, and there was no way he could drive Wheeler's car—a Volkswagen Rabbit—away from the scene.

Certain that the attention of the waiting motorists was

on the police cars and ambulances ahead, Carter vaulted over the guardrail and slipped into the Rabbit. He had guessed right; Wheeler had left the keys in the ignition. Carter eased behind the wheel and slid down until he couldn't be seen from outside.

In that quiet moment, he recalled the charred face of the man who had saved his life—probably twice—and he let the tears come. He felt no shame.

Ten minutes later, the police decided to let the traffic flow again. Carter fired up the Rabbit's engine, turned on his left blinker, and bulled his way into the line of traffic. At the first crossover, he made a U-turn and headed toward Amsterdam.

Carter was calculating the time as he drove rapidly north. Anatoly Gritchkin would be sending someone to find out what happened to the men in the Renault. Since the Russian would be preoccupied with the house specialty at Chez Carlo, he'd be in no special hurry to do much of anything. Carter could count on perhaps an hour of grace there.

If Gritchkin learned in an hour of what had happened on the highway, it would take him another thirty minutes to determine that his ambush had wiped out the wrong man. He would know that the American who had faced him nose-to-nose on Aeroflot Flight 9 to Moscow was still alive and kicking, and planning to stop him from taking that particular flight again.

Gritchkin would either change his plans by taking another flight, or he'd make a beeline for Schiphol Airport and hide out aboard the plane until the mechanics made it airworthy.

Using such logic, Nick Carter laid his own plans.

He would use that hour and a half to best advantage. He'd eliminate whatever danger Tammi might face, get his head looked after by a medical expert, report to Hawk about what had happened down in that ravine, and be waiting for Anatoly Gritchkin and his goons at Schiphol.

How he'd get the briefcase away from Gritchkin, he had no idea. But after seeing the awful face of Jonathan Wheeler, the prospect of chopping off Gritchkin's hand to obtain the briefcase had a rather special appeal to him.

Carter's hunch about Tammi Krisler was correct. When Aleksi Veronovitch had been assigned by Boris Stanislav to check out the house in the exclusive Buitenveldert section, he had thoughtfully provided Veronovitch with a backup. The agent, who had been among the massive guard contingent at the Nederlands Hilton, had arrived at the house across the street from Tammi Krisler two hours after Veronovitch had been killed by Jonathan Wheeler.

The Russian agent's name was Josef Petrosky. He was tall and thin, with a brown mustache that resembled a dirty toothbrush, and with startlingly white teeth of which he was quite proud. He had been smiling, showing those glittering teeth, when he came out onto the flat roof and found his comrade slumped behind the low wall where he had been lying in wait for Nick Carter.

"I hope you're only pretending to be asleep, Aleksi," Josef said as he leaned down to show his partner his shining smile. "Comrade Stanislav may be dead, but his ghost will come back to get you for sleeping on duty."

The smile faded and died when Josef Petrosky realized that not only was Aleksi Veronovitch not asleep, but that he, Josef, had two ghosts to deal with now—Aleksi's and their former superior's.

Petrosky's first emotion was fear. He wheeled around on the roof, looking for potential unseen enemies, for the barrels of guns. He was alone, except for Veronovitch and his ghost.

The slim agent leaned closer and saw that Veronovitch

still held the big Weatherby Mark V that Stanislav had provided as a sniper's weapon. The gun was aimed at the house across the street. Without moving the rifle, Josef Petrosky leaned down to peer through the powerful Bausch & Lomb scope.

He saw a bedroom window of the house across the street and far back in the tall trees. The bedroom was empty, but a pale pinkish light revealed that the bed was rumpled as though someone had been sleeping or carousing there. He pursed his lips, showed his teeth again, and gazed at the dead Veronovitch.

"I don't know if you were paying attention to duty, Aleksi," he said, "or turning into a peeping Tom. Either way, I'd better find out what was so interesting to you in that bedroom."

Slowly and quietly retracing his steps, Josef Petrosky went down into the house. He checked the basement to make certain that the man and woman who had lived there were still where Aleksi Veronovitch had put them after killing them, then slipped out the back door.

In a roundabout way, he slinked across the street to the home of Tammi Krisler.

Even though darkness had come some time ago, Tammi wasn't due at the Nieuw Gudens nightclub for another two hours. She wasn't a supper-club singer. She entertained the big spenders who drank the expensive (but watered) champagne, pinched the buxom cocktail waitresses, and spent fortunes in tips trying to stump the Dutch band by requesting American tunes from the swing era. Such customers, usually international executives and playboys, were always shocked to learn that the club's band could imitate Tommy Dorsey's famous "Boogie-Woogie." They didn't know, of course, that many of the doddering old guys in the band's back row had played for Tommy, and even for his brother Jimmy.

They layed out fat bets that the band couldn't play T. Dorsey's theme song or Vaughan Monroe's "Racing With the Moon." They always lost those fat bets, and the band members delightedly split them equally, including Tammi because she had to imitate American female vocalists and remember all the lyrics.

At the moment that Nick Carter was maneuvering the little VW Rabbit into the city and Josef Petrosky was picking the lock on the front door, Tammi Krisler was in the upstairs shower, washing away the remnants of her lovemaking with Carter and the nap that she'd taken when he'd gone off to seek out the bad guys.

She was singing Kay Starr's "Bonapart's Retreat" when the sliding door of the shower stall was ripped off its track.

She instinctively covered her breasts and crotch with her hands as she stared at the leering man with the mouthful of glittering teeth. She also let out a scream, which only made the man grin more pleasurably.

"Nice pretty lady," Josef Petrosky said in terrible Dutch. "We go bed now, yes?"

Either Tammi's instincts were better than the Russian's, or his fascination with her naked body was too much for him. Whichever, she leaped so suddenly from the shower at the tall, thin man with the toothbrush mustache that Petrosky had no time to react. Tammi hit him with her hands clasped into a club. She followed with a wicked twist of her hips that slammed the Russian back into the wall. She heard the *clunk* as his head struck the hard tile.

She was backing off for a second attack when Petrosky gained his wits and put up defenses. Tammi's next blow struck bony arms; her hips missed Petrosky's sidestepping body, and she crashed into the tile wall.

She cursed as pain shot through her naked, soap-covered body.

"Good fighter, good lover," Petrosky said in Russian, his smile back.

And then he closed hands that had a viselike grip over Tammi Krisler's flailing wrists and began to drag her from the bathroom. He threw her onto the rumpled bed he had seen through his comrade's rifle scope. When Tammi came up fighting again, Josef Petrosky lost his temper.

He coldcocked her with a right cross. When his fist met her jaw, the sound of it flooded the big empty house. The next sound to reach the downstairs rooms was a soft one, that of Tammi Krisler's naked, helpless body falling unconscious onto the bed.

Josef Petrosky walked around the bed, observing the woman from every angle. He prodded here and there with an outstretched finger. Then, satisfied that he would have his way with this woman, and that she would probably come to at the proper moment and be pleasantly surprised by his sexual abilities, he unbuckled his belt and dropped his trousers.

And all the while those teeth shone like phosphorus in the dimly lighted bedroom.

Carter left the Rabbit a block from Tammi's house and walked up the sloping street, keeping close to walls and shrubbery. If his hunch were correct and the Russians had Tammi's house staked out, the man on stakeout would be nervous now that it was dark. The man would have a tight, itchy finger on whatever trigger he held in his grip.

The man from AXE stopped long enough to get a fair make on the yard and house across from Tammi's plush place. The house was dark, looking at the same time ominous and innocent. Carter gave Tammi's house a similar casing, surprised that it was dark except for her bedroom. She should be almost ready to go to work by now. Surely she'd have come downstairs to prepare dinner or a snack.

Carter's almost infallible sixth sense warned him that Tammi might be in danger. There was something about her house that troubled him. He stared at the bedroom window and the pale pink light that barely broke the darkness outside the window. No shadows moved up there; all was quiet.

It wasn't that Carter ignored the warning signal that was tolling like a distant bell in the back of his mind. It was a matter of priorities. If Tammi were in trouble, then the one or more Russian agents who were in the house across the street were watching to see who might come to her rescue. It was important, then, to take out the interference before dashing in like gangbusters and getting his ass shot off. He had been doing the gangbusters bit all along; now was the time for finesse, even caution.

Carter eased through a hedge and crawled over a fence and moved like a shadow across the lawn of the house across from Tammi's.

The house was big, and three stories high. The front section of roof was flat, but Carter guessed that there was a low wall up there and that a sniper could well be hiding behind that wall. He moved in closer, and sure enough, there was the barrel of a rifle sticking out over the edge of the roof.

Ducking quickly back toward the house to avoid being seen, Carter reconnoitered the house and, to his surprise, found the front door unlocked. A smart stakeout, he knew, would lock all doors and give himself that small extra edge of getting prepared when someone tried to force them open. Either this stakeout wasn't smart, or he had a partner who was guarding that unlocked door. Or—hell, it was anybody's guess. Carter had to take a chance and go through that unlocked door.

On the small porch, Carter eased behind a tall wooden column and gazed back across the street toward Tammi's house. There was still that pale light in her bedroom, but he could see only the ceiling of the room from his present position. The sniper on the roof above, however, no doubt had a clear look at everything in that room. Carter recalled the afternoon's lovemaking and knew that the man on the roof had seen that. He'd also seen Carter leave and get into the red Volvo.

There had been that moment, Carter recalled, when he felt a great sense of danger, even of impending death. The sensation had come strongly, then had died. Why? What had changed things? Had the sniper been prepared to shoot him but changed his mind at the last minute? Or, as Carter had originally guessed, had Jonathan Wheeler, the AXE agent assigned by Hawk, taken out the sniper? No, the sniper was still there—or, at least, *some* sniper was still there.

Carter decided that guessing was getting him nowhere fast, so he went to the door of the dark house and turned the knob, slowly, very slowly. He released the knob and waited, just in case a booby trap had been attached to a timer. He backed away from the door and waited for an explosion to blow it off its hinges.

There was no explosion, no sound at all, not even a neighborhood dog barking at phantoms.

Carter opened the door even more slowly than he had turned the knob. He left it standing open while he pressed his body against the wall of the house. His Luger was in his right hand, and as he waited to see if a timed booby trap might go off as a result of the door being opened, he saw from a spill of light from the street that the gridlike grip of the weapon was smeared with dried blood.

The wound on Carter's head had stopped seeping blood, but he still looked like an escapee from a battlefield. He had felt faint a couple of times during the drive up from Antwerp, but he still put off the matter of medical help. When he could be certain that Tammi was all right, he'd get the head wound patched up and he'd check in with Hawk to tell him about Wheeler.

But the dried blood on Wilhelmina's grip reminded Carter that he had a lot of ground to cover this night, many things to do. In the heat of battle, and in the wild series of events and misadventures, he'd almost forgotten his main objective: retrieving the valuable data on America's White Horse project.

Well, he'd have to put that on the back burner one more time. Right now, unless his senses deceived him, there was a sniper on the roof of this house and he had his rifle aimed at the pink light coming from Tammi Krisler's bedroom window.

Once inside the house, Carter closed the door and then stood silently in blackness. He allowed two full minutes for a booby-trap timer to react, or for the sniper's partner to make his move. When nothing happened, he had the horrible feeling that he was on a fool's errand here, perhaps even entering another trap.

The rifle on the roof could be just that—a rifle with no rifleman behind it. This house could be empty. The Russian stakeout, if any, could have gone over to Tammi's house right after Carter had left earlier. She could be in great danger, as he'd guessed down in that ravine when he learned of the existence of Jonathan Wheeler. Or, and he hated to let the thought come to the surface, she could be dead.

Carter decided that he was being too cautious. He moved through the house quickly now, seeking clues as to whether it had been used as a stakeout, or was at this moment occupied by alien and enemy forces. In the basement, his worst fears were confirmed when he found the bodies of an elderly man and woman. He had gone to the basement as a matter of course, to make sure that the house was clean before he confronted the sniper—or possible sniper—on the roof.

Caution returned to Carter's M.O. as he moved up from the basement and checked out the three floors of the enormous house. *Christ,* he thought, *why couldn't Tammi live in a poor section where the houses were smaller and easier to search?*

Carter found small signs of alien occupancy: a cigarette butt crushed out barbarically on a hall carpet; traces of urine alongside a toilet where a careless Russian had taken a leak; a ring in a bathtub where someone dirty—and also careless—had taken a bath; a small bedroom table laden with Styrofoam cups that had once held coffee. On the staircase leading to the roof, he found a paper bag and, opening it with utmost care, found the bony, greasy remnants of a chicken dinner from a famous American restaurant chain that now had outlets all over the civilized world. He sighed as he thought of that word, "civilized." In a civilized world, Carter mused, the mere idea of having weapons that could cause that world to be instantly obliterated would be thought utterly ridiculous. Carter set aside the paper bag of chicken bones and moved up the narrow staircase to the roof.

When he reached a central chimney and peered around it, he saw the sniper at the base of the wall on the flat front roof. He watched for a full minute and saw no movement. Beyond, through the trees, he could see the faint beacon of Tammi Krisler's bedroom window. The pounding in his head, a pounding that had let up during the drive from Antwerp, returned, and he thought he would pass out from the pain.

He waited another minute. The pain eased. And the sniper at the edge of the roof still hadn't moved. Time, Carter decided, was being wasted in very large dollops.

Deciding on action, he took a single 9mm cartridge from a Luger clip in his jacket pocket. He tossed it in a high arc through the dark air and heard it land with a *ping* far out on the roof, within inches of the silent, motionless sniper.

The sniper didn't moved a muscle. Either he had nerves of steel, or he was dead.

Dead.

The word resonated in Carter's head like an echo in a canyon, or a shout for help in a mausoleum.

He felt like shouting himself, of screaming out all the obscenities and curses he had learned in a long and some-what checkered life on the trail of his country's enemies. Dammit to hell, he'd been had! While he was following a false and dead trail, terrible things could have been happening—or had already happened—to dear, sweet, beautiful Tammi Krisler.

Carter was angry, but virtually all of the anger was directed at himself.

There was no solace in knowing that he had been working against two master spies—Boris Stanislav and Anatoly Gritchkin—and the combined intelligence of the entire KGB. There was no solace in knowing that he couldn't be in two places at once: on the trail of Gritchkin *and* here to protect Tammi.

There was, instead, anger and frustration and a fury that knew no bounds. So far, even though he'd enjoyed a few brief victories, all the ass-kicking had been one-sided. His ass was the one being kicked around the block by the combined efforts of a spy who was now dead and one who was enamored of Amazons.

Henceforth, Nick Carter decided, *he* would do all the ass-kicking, and the Russians would be the targets. He would start with the dead sniper at the edge of the roof.

Carter stomped across the roof and hoped that the sniper really was alive and would turn around. The Killmaster had Wilhelmina ready to blow the man's head into a billion bloody pieces. But the man didn't turn; he was dead, as Carter had figured.

Carter had drawn back his right foot, prepared to kick the dead Russian off the roof, when the same thought that had struck the man named Josef Petrosky came to Carter. He stared at the dead man and at the angle of the rifle barrel. He saw that it was pointed directly toward Tammi Krisler's window.

Instead of leaning close to the dead man to look through the scope, Carter yanked the rifle out of the man's grip. He admired the big Weatherby for a fraction of a second, then homed the scope in on Tammi Krisler's window.

What he saw broke the dam of suppressed anger.

There, on that dark roof, Nick Carter put voice to that abundant panoply of expletives he had been storing up all his adult life.

TWELVE

Carter's first impulse was to blast away at the tall, thin man who loomed above Tammi Krisler on the big bed.

The man was kneeling between her legs, and a large set of gleaming white teeth grinned down at the woman. In his hand was a small revolver that he was pointing more or less in the direction of Tammi's head. The idea, Carter supposed, was that if she didn't cooperate, he would blow her brains out.

Carter backed off from his first impulse. From that great distance, he had no guarantee that the heavy slugs from the Weatherby would strike the man and miss the woman. The slugs would have to penetrate the glass of the window. If only one bullet were deflected in her direction, Carter's anger would once again have defeated him.

And yet he couldn't just stand there and do nothing. The seconds seemed to move like minutes as he thought of what to do. If he fired at the downstairs windows, he would frighten the man off and save Tammi from being raped. And frightening off the man wasn't what Carter wanted. He wanted to catch that man if he could. He wanted to question him and find out just what the hell was going on.

It had puzzled Carter when the five men came at dawn

to blow him and Tammi away, only to be blown away themselves. It had puzzled him even more to learn that one, and then two, men had been assigned to stake out Tammi's house long after that dawn raid had backfired for the Russians.

He couldn't believe that Anatoly Gritchkin had ordered the men to watch the house. The spy seemed intent only on getting back to Moscow and, failing that, on seeing as much as he could of the decadent West.

The answer came. Carter could achieve two purposes with one decisive act. There remained the gamble of a possible deflected bullet and flying glass, but Carter had learned years ago that there was a gamble in any decisive act, and certainly those that were violent.

He raised the Weatherby slightly and aimed at the upper part of the window, where the shade would stop glass from flying all over the room. Or so he hoped. The bullets, if they went true, would embed themselves in a far wall, high above the bed where Tammi Krisler lay.

Carter also didn't want to kill the skinny Russian. He wanted to scare the man away from Tammi, but he also wanted him to know that the bullets had come from his dead comrade's perch on the roof across the street. If Carter had the Russian agent's mentality figured correctly, the man would scamper out the back way as soon as the bullets started flying, then would circle back in the darkness and head for the house where Carter was now perched on the roof.

There would be one slight alteration in positions. Carter wouldn't wait for the man on the roof. He'd catch him as soon as he crossed the street, and he'd get the answers he sought or know the reason why.

Without further hesitation, because the Russian agent was now lowering his body toard a vainly struggling Tammi, Carter squeezed the trigger of the Weatherby and didn't let up as the heavy rifle bucked and swayed in his grip.

The Russian named Aleksi Veronovitch had equipped the big rifle with a noise abater, but it was hardly silent. The *rap-rap-rap* sounds of the cartridges exploding in the breech filled the quiet street. The sound, Carter was happy to note, was no louder than if a man happened to be striking a car fender with a claw hammer.

All hell must have broken loose in that pink bedroom across the wide boulevard. Carter thought he heard a scream, but he couldn't be certain. He hoped he had; a scream from Tammi indicated that she had survived the hail of bullets from the Weatherby. But the pink light that had bled faintly into the night was gone now; the whole house was dark.

Carter was certain that the Russian had long since fled the pink bedroom in which the dim light had been shattered by the copper-sheathed missiles. The man was making his way downstairs now, seeking the back door. With calm deliberation, Carter nestled the dead man back in place behind the low rampart, but he did not replace the rifle on top of the wall. Instead he placed one of the dead man's hands on the ledge and let it dangle over the side, then tossed the Weatherby, empty now, back across the flat roof.

He went back down the narrow staircase, angrily kicked the bag of chicken bones down the hallway, and moved through darkness to the front door. He checked through a tiny window to make certain the agent from across the street wasn't watching, then slipped outside. He leaped from the low porch into the shrubbery and made his way in short bursts across the dark, shadowed lawn to the main gate.

From that vantage point, he had a clear view of the hedge and fence that surrounded the property. When the

Russian came across, he'd have to penetrate the hedge and climb the fence, and Carter would have a make on him.

He waited. Ten minutes passed, and he began to despair that his plan hadn't worked. Maybe the guy had skipped out altogether and was right now dredging up reinforcements. Then again maybe the son of a bitch was still in Tammi's house, raping her up there in the dark bedroom. No, he decided. Not even the horniest man in the world could continue the act of sex after the room in which he was committing it had been taken apart by a big Weatherby Mark V.

Carter continued to wait. In ten more minutes his patience was rewarded. A shadow moved alongside the fence and hedge fifty yards to his right. Carter moved in that direction, in a crouch, alongside the base of the steel fence.

The man with the shiny teeth came out of the shadows and made a rush for the house that Carter had vacated. The man stopped in the center of the yard and gazed up toward the roof where the sniper had lain in wait. Carter chose that moment, while the Russian was puzzling over that dead and dangling hand, to make his move.

In a burst of silent speed, he shot across the lawn and downed the Russian with a flying tackle. There were double groans as the two men hit the ground. Carter gave the man no chance to fight. He came out of the melee with his stiletto in his hand. He grasped the Russian's shirt collar with his left hand and touched the tip of the slender steel blade to the man's soft underchin.

"I don't know if you understand English, pal," Carter hissed there on the dark lawn, "but you'll understand this: one false move and I'll push this blade straight up into your brain. Now, tell me if you speak English!"

The man nodded and Carter was relieved. He spoke Russian well, but he needed information fast and accurate. There were too many nuances of meaning in various Russian words, and he had no time for games.

"Speaking English very good," Josef Petrosky babbled as he tried to screw his eyeballs down to get a look at the sharp object poking into his flesh. "Only coming here to see girl friend and to have good time. Why you me knocking down?"

Carter groaned. He'd have to speak Russian after all. The man's English was about twenty notches below Carter's Russian.

Josef Petrosky claimed to be a Russian diplomat assigned to the protection of the people in the house across from Tammi Krisler's.

"They are also Russian diplomats," Petrosky said in Ukrainian Russian. "There has been trouble in the neighborhood, and I was assigned to keep them from harm. Surely you can understand why I was moving so cautiously across the yard."

"Yeah," Carter said, keeping the man's face close to his. "Would you explain why the people who live here have been murdered and trussed up like butchered cows in the cellar? And why is that man on the roof dead with a bullet in his head?"

Petrosky went silent. Carter moved Hugo's blade a fraction of an inch. A bead of blood appeared on Petrosky's chin. The Russian yelped but did not move. The smile that had grown as he lied through his shiny teeth was long since dead. He gazed at Carter, begging with his pale blue eyes for mercy. The idea of mercy gave Carter an idea.

"Come on," he said, easing back on the stiletto and yanking the man to his feet. "Your fate is out of my hands now. Let's go across the street and let a certain lady friend decide what's to be done with you."

Josef Petrosky was so frightened of what might happen

next that he made no attempt to break the grip of steel on his arms and upper torso. He remembered the battle with the woman in the shower, how she had nearly knocked him unconscious with a judo chop and a wicked slam against the tile wall. After what he had done to her, how could he expect mercy? He was afraid of what was to come, but he was equally afraid that this big American with the little knife might fulfill his promise and drive the blade deep into his brain. He went peacefully to his doom.

In the dark bedroom, Carter found an unshattered lamp and turned it on. Tammi Krisler was hovered against the bedpost, her pink sheets pulled up to her chin. She was trembling all over.

"Nicholas!" she cried. "Oh, Nicholas, you have come to save me! But why did you bring that animal in here? I want him out! And what has happened to you, Nicholas? Why are you so bloody?"

"It's okay, Tammi. Everything'll be alright," Carter said soothingly. "Don't worry about me."

He helped Tammi into the bathroom to bathe. Carter then tied Petrosky to one of the posts of Tammi's bed.

When Tammi returned, wrapped in a robe, the look of fury on her face when she saw the Russian answered all the questions in Carter's mind. Yes, the man had succeeded in raping her before Carter showed up to stop him. What else he had done, Carter was soon to learn.

"I need your help, Tammi," Carter told her as she regarded the skinny Russian with open hatred. "I've asked this guy a few questions that need answering, but he merely lies through those nice-guy teeth. I figure you owe him a few licks, so maybe you'd like to help me conduct a little inquiry."

"With pleasure," Tammi said, smiling for the first time. "But I need the little pistol he had with him."

"Right here," Carter said, taking a .32-caliber revolver from his jacket pocket. He had slipped it from the
Russian's pocket when he'd taken him down with that
flying tackle. Rule one was to disarm your man even as
you were striking the first blow.

Tammi took the pistol and checked to see that it was
loaded. She removed all the bullets but one, then snapped
the cylinder back in place. She spun the cylinder.

"I'm going to play a little game," she said. "It's not
quite the same as the one you played with me, but I think it
will serve the purpose."

As she spoke, she aimed the pistol at Josef Petrosky's
head at point-blank range. Carter got the picture and knew
that the man had played a sick variation of Russian
roulette with Tammi. When Tammi drew back the hammer of the .32, Carter asked his first question:

"Are you KGB?"

"*Nyet,*" the Russian said, shaking his head.

Tammi pulled the trigger.

There was no shot, but there might as well have been.
Josef Petrosky let out an ear-piercing scream. His whole
body thrashed on the bed as he tried to get out of the way of
the lethal little gun. Tammi merely smiled and cocked the
hammer again. Carter held up the game long enough to
stuff a hand towel into the Russian's mouth. No sense
giving the neighbors cause to call the police again.

"Are you a KGB agent?" Carter asked again.

Tammi didn't have to pull the trigger again. She was
very disappointed. And very angry. And once, when Josef
Petrosky hesitated slightly in answering a question from
the Killmaster, she let revenge rule her thinking and
pulled it anyhow. Petrosky went wild on the bed, even
though the gun again didn't fire. When Tammi cocked the
hammer again, greatly enhancing the odds that the next

pull of the trigger would sent a hot pellet of lead into his temple there was no doubt that the cooperation and truthfulness of Josef Petrosky would be complete.

Over the next several minutes, Nick Carter learned how Boris Stanislav, acting independently of Anatoly Gritchkin—in fact, even *against* Gritchkin's knowledge or permission—had tried to protect the foolish master spy. Gritchkin, as Carter had guessed, had placed his peculiar sexual desires above the call of duty—at least, that was the opinion of the late Boris Stanislav.

Stanislav had arranged for the large guard contingent at the Nederlands Hilton. He had arranged for Aleksi Veronovitch to kill the old couple in the house across the street and to wait for the perfect time to kill the American agent who had been on the trail of Anatoly Gritchkin.

Petrosky, Carter learned, knew nothing of the contents of the briefcase. He knew only that it was so important that he and other agents had been told that, to make certain it reached Moscow, no effort was to be spared. If necessary, Petrosky told Carter and Tammi, Gritchkin himself would be killed to make certain that the briefcase reached the Soviet Union.

Then why, Carter asked, hadn't the Russians arranged to have a special plane sent in to pick up Gritchkin and the briefcase?

"Well, you have to understand certain things," Petrosky said. "If we made a big fuss and set up special arrangements, it would bring an army of American agents to stop Gritchkin."

"Makes sense," Carter said, grinning down at the terrified man. "It also makes sense that Aeroflot simply doesn't have any other planes to send, right?"

Petrosky grinned back, but only briefly. "Right, comrade."

The Russian agent's information was initially of little help to Carter. The man knew only that Veronovitch had been given his assignment by Boris Stanislav, and that he, Petrosky, had been assigned to keep watch over Veronovitch and to relieve him. When he had found Veronovitch dead, and knew already that Stanislav was dead, he succumbed to his own sexual desires and went after Tammi.

Although Petrosky knew nothing of the whereabouts of Anatoly Gritchkin, and nothing of his plans, he did know that a heavy security contingent would be on hand at the airport when the man returned.

"Orders came from Moscow," Petrosky said. "When Comrade Gritchkin returns to Schiphol Airport, there will be twenty well-armed men to guard him. The aircraft will not carry commercial passengers. It will be used only to take Comrade Gritchkin and his armed escort to Moscow."

This was not good news to Nick Carter. He had no specific plan in mind to get that briefcase from Gritchkin, but it was obvious that a guard contingent of twenty men would frustrate any plans he might devise. Since his failure to snatch the briefcase while playing the role of a Dutch businessman, Carter had been playing the game on a minute-by-minute basis, rolling with the punches, keeping tabs on the target but unable to formulate any hard-and-fast plan of action.

Such a plan was obviously needed now, and he had no such plan. He could notify Hawk that Gritchkin would have a huge bodyguard contingent and ask that drastic and forceful action be taken to stop the man from leaving for Moscow, but he knew what Hawk's answer would be. It was N3's job to stop Gritchkin; N3 would have to get his act together and do his job.

The really infuriating part to Carter was the fact that he had actually had his hands on that precious briefcase, had been nose-to-nose with Anatoly Gritchkin. Although the thought had occurred to him to use Hugo to cut the handcuffs from the agent's wrist—or, better yet, to cut off the man's hand at the wrist—there was something in his nature that cried out against performing such grisly acts.

"Well, Nicholas?" Tammi said as her hand moved anxiously on the pistol and she held it even closer to Josef Petrosky's temple. "What's next? Any more questions?"

"No. No more questions."

"Want me to shoot him?" Tammi asked. "He'll make an unholy mess of my bed, but I don't care. I'm buying a new one, anyway. I wouldn't sleep in this bed again for a million dollars."

"No, please," Petrosky begged, his eyes bugging out. "I can be of help to you."

"In what way?" Carter asked. He felt dizzy and slightly queasy.

Petrosky began to babble about how he had wanted to defect for years because his life in Russia was so rotten and his superiors were so stupid and insensitive. For political asylum in the United States, he would work with Carter, get false messages to Anatoly Gritchkin, lead the master spy into Carter's trap for a change.

"I don't have a trap for Gritchkin," Carter said, watching the man closely to gauge the degree of his despair. "How would you suggest I set a trap for him?" The dizziness grew.

"I could call him and tell him that I have captured you," Petrosky said, his eyes flitting from Tammi's nervous hand to Carter's grim face. "You and the woman and several of your agents could be waiting. When he arrived in his big limousine, you could kill him, cut off his hand, and take the briefcase. I ask only—"

"Nicholas!" Tammi's voice cut through the room. "What is wrong with you?"

Carter had been listening to the skinny agent try to weasel his way out of trouble. When the first two waves of dizziness came, he'd succeeded in ignoring the discomfort. But the third and fourth waves were overwhelming. He felt the room begin to sway, then he heard Petrosky's whining voice fade off as though it were disappearing down a well.

He wasn't even aware that he was falling. He never heard Tammi Krisler's anxious cries. He never felt the impact when he crashed to the floor.

Tammi dropped the pistol and dashed around the bed to help Nick Carter. He looked terrible, and she had wanted to call a doctor as soon as she had seen him, but her anger at the skinny Russian had overcome her good sense. Now Carter was pale as chalk.

As Tammi was taking Carter's pulse, she heard the Russian begin to move about on the bed. She raised her head just in time to see Petrosky work his right hand free of the sheet that had held it. The Russian's hand flashed out, seeking the revolver that Tammi had dropped onto the bed.

"You son of a bitch!" Tammi cried.

She flew at the Russian with more fury than she'd used when she'd flown from the shower when the man first came to her room. She clasped her hands together, and just as Petrosky's hand was closing on the revolver, Tammi brought her hands down toward his crotch.

Petrosky pulled the trigger while Tammi was staring down the barrel of the pistol.

There was a click.

Then there was a crunch and a wild grunt as Tammi's clasped hands slammed into the agent's crotch. Petrosky grunted again and again, his hand going limp on the pistol.

He was just regaining his senses and tightening his grip on the gun when Tammi grabbed it and yanked it from his fingers.

With cold fury and calm efficiency, she put the barrel of the revolver to Josef Petrosky's temple and pulled the trigger.

The hammer struck the solitary cartridge in the cylinder. The charge of gunpowder exploded like thunder in the room.

Tammi Krisler kept her eyes on the incredible scene before her, fascinated by the halo of blood, bones, and hair that sprayed out from the opposite side of Josef Petrosky's head.

Tammi watched as the agent bucked on the bed. Her eyes never left that tall, skinny, dying body until the flood of blood stopped surging from the enormous hole in the man's head and the muscles stopped jerking.

Then, revolted, she threw the gun across the room and dashed once more for the bathroom, where she lost what remained of her lunch.

Returning to the room, Tammi drew a blanket over the dead man and went to Nick Carter's side. His pulse was strong, but his face remained pale and pasty.

Tammi Krisler went to her bedside telephone, calmly wiped blood and brains from the receiver, and called a physician she knew, a man who could be trusted, a man who would not ask questions or make unnecessary reports to the efficient Dutch police.

And then she sat on the floor beside the unconscious Nick Carter and cried with great, gulping sobs.

THIRTEEN

He awoke to a gentle pressure on his cheek. The pounding in his head was gone, replaced by a sense of wellbeing, of floating. He knew that he'd been given a shot for pain, or, if the Russian agent had somehow won out, an overdose of drugs. He opened his eyes.

"Welcome back," the bearded man above him said in gentle Dutch. "I was just touching up a few places with antiseptic. You look as though you lost a fight with a pack of jackals, my friend."

"Who are you?" Nick Carter asked. He looked around the room, but he didn't recognize it. He wasn't in a hospital, and he certainly wasn't in Tammi Krisler's bedroom. He was in a dining room, on the table, naked.

"Doctor No-Name," the bearded man said. "Best you know nothing more than that. I was sent for, I came, I stitched up a nasty gash in your head, and now I must go. You never saw me. Good-bye, my friend. Have those stitches taken out in ten days."

Nick Carter slowly swung his legs over the table and sat up as the doctor, a tall, heavy man with a slight stoop, picked up a black satchel and walked out of the room. Carter recognized the room now; it was Tammi Krisler's dining room. He was battling dizziness when Tammi walked into the room with a tray.

"Off the table, Nicholas," she ordered. "The doctor says you are going to be fine but that you can use a good meal. Goodness, don't they let you eat in your line of work? I can count your ribs."

Carter couldn't remember when he had eaten last, but he sensed that a part of his weakness and dizziness stemmed from hunger. He slipped from the table and gazed at Tammi as she spread a feast of steak, potatoes, spinach, salad, and fresh fruit before him. Carter looked at his watch. It was late.

"Shouldn't you be at work?" he asked.

Tammi burst into laughter. "My God, Nicholas! After all the crazy things that have happened in this house in the past twenty-four hours, and all that has happened to you, the only question you can ask is why I am not at work? Silly fool, I called to say I was sick. When I called to say that, I really was sick. I had just killed a man."

Memories of those final moments in Tammi's bedroom filtered slowly into Carter's Demerol-clogged brain.

"Tell me about it," he said, remembering that he had passed out with Josef Petrosky tied up on the bed and Tammi with the little pistol jammed into the agent's privates. As Tammi talked, relating how she had nearly been killed and had finally shot the Russian in the head, Carter got dressed and slowly ate his food and slowly regained strength.

"This hasn't been one of my better visits to your home," he finally said by way of apology. "I promise to be a better guest next time. But how did I get down here? And where is Petrosky?"

"I carried you down here," she said, "because I didn't want either of us to stay in that bedroom another minute. I also didn't want the doctor to see all those bullet holes upstairs. He is a man I trust, but he is also a man I like. The less he has to keep secret, the better.''

"What he doesn't know won't hurt him, right?"

"Right."

"I can understand that," Carter said as he chewed the delicious meat and felt the Demerol ease the soreness in his body and keep the pounding in his head to a tolerable level. "You still haven't told me where Petrosky is.''

Tammi shrugged, but Carter knew that she was troubled by what had happened up in that bedroom. "I left him there. In a few minutes, I will leave this house. I will return in two hours. When I return, I don't wish to see any sign of that man. I don't know who you work for, Nicholas, but I know that you have some kind of organization with tremendous resources—what you Americans call clout. I want you to use your clout to clean up my place and remove that man's body from my bedroom. The sooner that happens, the sooner I may be able to forget this terrible day and night.''

"It hasn't *all* been bad," Carter said, grinning as he shoved in a hunk of potato that had been drowned in sour cream. "Has it?"

"There were moments . . ." Tammi said, permitting herself a small smile. "I cannot lie about the fact that there were sweet moments.''

"And there will be sweet moments again?"

"Of course," Tammi said. She bent to kiss his cheek, careful to pick a spot that hadn't been bruised or scratched during Carter's wild plunge into the ravine near Antwerp. "Meanwhile, I mean what I say. I will leave now, and I expect to return to an immaculate house.''

Carter watched her go, watched that marvelous swaying of her hips. He listened as doors were opened and closed and as the big engine of the powerful Mercedes was fired up. He heard the car's engine die away as Tammi Krisler drove off into the night.

He continued eating, dreading the necessary call to Hawk but happy that a plan was beginning to hatch in his head. It wasn't the greatest of plans, he had to admit, but it was a plan.

The rough, gruff voice boomed over the transatlantic connection.

"Good Lord, N3, what kind of foolishness are you up to over there? I ask you to stop one man and take his briefcase away, and you keep calling with ridiculous problems. Just how many bodies do you have stashed, and where are they?"

Carter felt almost comforted by David Hawk's familiar griping. He could see his chief, a cheap black cigar clamped between stained teeth, his hand gripping the telephone receiver as though trying to choke it to death, his steely eyes riveted on the bare wall opposite his desk in his office on Washington's Dupont Circle.

"I wish you had told me about the man you sent to back me up," Carter said by way of response. "We could have worked together."

"Tell me about this man," Hawk demanded. He wouldn't admit that he had assigned a man to cover N3, but Carter could tell by the tone of his boss's voice that he was keenly interested in what might have happened to Jonathan Wheeler. Hawk cared deeply for all of AXE's employees.

Carter told Hawk how Jonathan Wheeler had twice saved his life, then had died because he had failed to duck quickly enough when the gasoline tank of the red Volvo exploded.

''I know it sounds hard to believe that he would die and that I would escape with minor injuries and burns,'' Carter said, ''but you have to understand the intensity of that explosion and its effect on anything or anyone standing or sitting. The three enemy agents were shredded. Our man was badly burned, but I'm convinced that death came when he was knocked back on his head. I was already flat, so I survived.''

''You've always been a survivor, N3,'' Hawk groused as though somehow blaming Carter for having lived through so many tight scrapes. ''All right, the police will take Wheeler's body to the nearest morgue, and our people will arrange to pick it up there. What's next on the agenda?''

Carter told of the old couple who lived across from Tammi Krisler. Tammi had said their name was Dussemann.

''I figured I would make an anonymous telephone tip to the Amsterdam police and let them try to figure out what happened over there,'' Carter suggested.

''The anonymous tip is a good idea,'' Hawk agreed, ''but do nothing until the matter of the briefcase is resolved. I don't want an investigation to cause any snags there. What next?''

Carter told of all the problems at Tammi's house, of the dead Russian agent up in Tammi's bed right now, and of her demand that things be put right within the next two hours.

Hawk exploded. ''You do try a man's patience, N3. All right, I'll arrange for a special team to clean up your mess at Miss Krisler's house, but I don't want you there when the team appears. What are your current plans for retrieving that briefcase?''

Carter told of the plan that was still unfolding in his

mind. Hawk listened quietly, then grunted.

"From that grunt," Carter said, "I surmise that you don't think much of the plan."

"Not much," Hawk responded, "but it's the only one you've got. Personally, I'd rather see you hotfoot it back to Antwerp and blow that Gritchkin character to kingdom come."

"I've already called Chez Carlo," Carter informed his boss. "The Russians left, much to the delight of the management, thirty minutes ago. They're on their way to Schiphol right now."

Hawk grunted again. "I suppose Gritchkin knows that twenty special guards are waiting for him at the aiport to see that he gets aboard that plane without interference from you or anyone else. That about the way you figure it?"

"No, sir," Carter said. "One of his men obviously was sent back to the scene of the ambush and reported that their three men and one of ours were killed. But the orders for the guard contingent just came from Moscow, according to Petrosky. I don't think Gritchkin knows that yet. It could work to our advantage."

"It damned well better," Hawk snapped. "Anything else?"

"Nothing else, sir. Just wish me luck."

"I've been wishing you luck," Hawk said. "So far, however, it hasn't done a hell of a lot of good. You're farther from the valuable data in that damned briefcase than ever. When I think that you actually had your hands on it, Nick, I could strangle you."

"You'd have to stand in line for that," Carter said with a sigh.

"I'm good at jumping to the heads of lines," Hawk

said, then hung up so swiftly that Carter was left holding a
dead phone. It was just as well; he had no topper for his
chief's final thrust.

Carter left Tammi Krisler's house and went to the
Dussemanns' to carry out the first step in his rather shaky
plan. Sensitive to the fact that two innocent old people lay
murdered in the basement and that a KGB agent was dead
on the roof, Carter used his tiny flashlight to dial the
telephone.

"Aeroflot," the ticket agent responded. Carter recognized the man's voice and rejoiced. It was the ticket agent
who had arranged to have the special wine aboard Flight 9
when Carter had boarded as Hans Vandergaard; it was the
man with the unlikely name of Pushkin whom Carter had
bribed, through Tammi, with three hundred guilders. It
was unlikely, Carter knew, that this man with the name of
one of Russia's finest writers would know of what had
happened to that expensive bottle of wine, or of anything
else that had happened on board the ill-fated flight.

"This is Heer Vandergaard," Carter said in Dutch.
"You were kind enough to reserve me a seat on Flight
Nine and to provide a bottle of Hintergarteen 'seventy-
five. Do you recall?"

"Ah, but of course, Heer Vandergaard," Pushkin replied, his voice growing more unctuous as he remembered
the three hundred guilders that had added greatly to his
defection funds. "I hope you found the wine to your
liking."

"Of course," Carter said, unwilling to tell the agent
that, as Hans Vandergaard, he had made a scene when the
steward had "ruined" the wine by improperly chilling it
and then warming it in the plane's microwave oven. "I

would like to ask that another bottle be reserved. I am assuming, of course, that Flight Nine will depart tomorrow.''

"Oh, no, sir," the agent named Pushkin said. "The flight will leave in exactly two hours, but there will be no regular passengers. For reasons I do not comprehend, the aircraft is being flown empty."

"No passengers, you say?"

"That is correct. The crew only."

"I see. Well, in that case, I suppose you have notified the regular passengers of this change and could not locate me."

There was a pause. "No, sir," Pushkin said. "We are under instructions not to call the passengers. The plane will simply leave in two hours—"

"There will be trouble," Carter said gruffly, interrupting the congenial agent. "I cannot believe that a responsible airline like Aeroflot would treat its passengers so shabbily."

During the next pause, Carter's mind worked swiftly. The news that the plane would leave without passengers jibed with what Petrosky had told him. It was important to Carter's plan, though, that the regular passengers be notified of the flight's departure time. He had to see to it that those passengers were notified.

"What you say is true," Pushkin agreed, "but what can be done?"

"Well, of course you must follow orders and not call them," Carter said, his voice full of sympathy for the agent's plight, "but who is to say that you cannot give me the names and telephone numbers of those passengers? I would take it upon myself to—"

"Oh, no, sir," the agent blurted. "If my superiors

learned that I gave you the names and numbers of Flight Nine's passengers, I would lose my job, perhaps even my life.''

"They won't learn of such a thing from me," Carter said. "In fact, I will tell the passengers that I am Hans Vandergaard and that I was at the airport and overheard your superiors discussing the fact that Flight Nine would leave without them. And for your trouble, there will be a special envelope left at your desk, as before, by the same lovely blond lady who left the last one. Inside that envelope will be ten thousand guilders.''

Carter held his breath. That amount of money would be more than enough for the agent to defect if he was of such a mind. It also should make him suspicious as to why a Dutch businessman would pay such an amount for seemingly unimportant information. Carter could only hope that the large amount of money would flood the ticket agent's mind and force him to suspend disbelief.

His hope was answered.

"If you have pencil and paper ready, Heer Vandergaard,'' the agent named Pushkin said, "I will read the names and telephone numbers.''

Ten minutes later, claiming to be Aeroflot agent Pushkin, Carter began calling the names on his list to tell them that Aeroflot Flight 9 would depart Schiphol Airport in one hour and fifty minutes. They were to report directly to the departure gate.

He felt guilty that he was no doubt costing the man named Pushkin his job, perhaps even his life, but he knew that he had no alternative.

The black limousine moved northward along Highway E-10, past Zevenbergen, Moerdijk, 's-Gravendeel,

Zwijndrecht and Ridderkerk. In the rear seat, alone, sat Anatoly Gritchkin, his mood blacker than the car in which he rode, blacker even than the night sky.

The call from his superior had come at an inopportune time. The Amazon and the men were at a critical point in their act, and he was just feeling the blissful effects of the third bottle of good champagne when the waiter summoned him. He had gone to the telephone with his two guards—the same two who were now in the front seat— and had listened to the harangue.

His good feelings had gone out the window.

That American agent, that clown who had outwitted them all by pretending to be a Dutch businessman, had not only escaped the trap Gritchkin had set for him, but he had taken out three excellent agents in the process. An American agent of some sort had been killed in the effort, but Gritchkin's superior assured him that the dead man in the ravine near Antwerp was not the same man seen at London's Heathrow Airport. And that man, the KGB boss said, was the same man who played the role of the Dutchman and came within a whisker of killing Anatoly Gritchkin aboard that stupid flight that had returned to Amsterdam instead of going on to Moscow.

To make matters worse, Gritchkin's boss had said, the American who was causing them all so much trouble was most assuredly on his way to Schiphol to await Gritchkin's arrival there. However, the boss assured the spy, twenty armed guards would meet Gritchkin on his arrival at Schiphol and would escort him to the plane that still waited at the same gate. The twenty guards would accompany Gritchkin to Moscow and right into the heart of the Kremlin.

Gritchkin had protested as he had listened to his superior and wished he would hurry so that he, Grichkin, could get back to the entertainment at Chez Carlo. He had insisted that he, alone, must deliver the important data in the briefcase that he still kept handcuffed to his wrist. How would it look on Gritchkin's long and glorious record if he was delivered to the gods of the Kremlin by twenty armed guard who would be nothing more than babysitters?

"I am thinking of how it would look," his superior had barked, "if the American put a bullet in your gut, cut off your hand, and took the briefcase to Washington. You will immediately leave that den of iniquity and return to Schiphol Airport. Is that understood, Comrade Gritchkin?"

"Understood," Gritchkin replied, gnashing his teeth.

"Immediately," his superior repeated. "Not after you have loitered at your table through another bottle of expensive champagne and another bout between the lady and the jackass. Immediately, Comrade Gritchkin, means now. *Now!*"

Before Gritchkin could offer further protest, his boss had hung up. He had muttered a few choice obscenities into the dead receiver, but he had obeyed orders by leaving Chez Carlo immediately in the black limousine.

When the limousine had passed the place on the highway where the three agents had sprung their trap on the American and had died in the vain effort, the driver had slowed. Police were directing traffic through a single lane while rescue equipment was bringing up the burned automobile and the charred bodies of the three Russians and the one American.

In that moment, furious with his situation and still rankling over the words and promises of his superior,

Anatoly Gritchkin pledged himself never to leave Amsterdam until the American who had been tracking him was dead.

He would never forget that moment in the airplane when the American's gun had gone off. The bullets had missed Gritchkin's head by a fraction of an inch and had punched through the Plexiglas window. And then the American had crashed the gun down onto Gritchkin's head.

The memory of that frightening and humiliating experience was sufficient motivation for Anatoly Gritchkin to disobey part of his superior's orders, and to make one last attempt to kill the American.

This time, he swore, he would not fail.

As the black limousine sped northward, the black mood began to dissipate, and Anatoly Gritchkin smiled to himself in the dark rear seat.

A plan was forming, an infallible plan.

FOURTEEN

As a simple act of decency, Nick Carter took blankets into the basement of the big house across from Tammi Krisler's house and spread them over the bodies of Mr. and Mrs. Dussemann. Even though the man on the roof was their murderer, Carter took a blanket up there and put it over the KGB agent.

But as Hawk had suggested, he didn't call the authorities to report that murders had occurred. He left the house and got into the Volkswagen Rabbit that Jonathan Wheeler had left above the ravine near Antwerp. He was pulling out of the driveway of the dark house when a van entered Tammi Krisler's driveway.

It was the special cleanup team dispatched by Hawk. Carter didn't wait to see who they were or what they would do. He drove slowly down the curving, tree-lined boulevard, heading for the main highway to Schiphol Airport.

His plan was too simple, he believed, for it to work. But he recalled from his studies of ancient military history that many of the best battle plans were the most simple.

Warriors as far back as Genghis Khan had learned and utilized the simple strategy of attacking when all common sense called for retreat. It was when an army was nearest to defeat that the opposing army became overconfident and relaxed its pressure. In that critical moment, Genghis Khan had learned, the opposing army became highly vulnerable. The last thing its generals expected was an attack. By the time they responded to the surprise assault, the presumably defeated army was already routing the ostensibly victorious one.

Carter did not consider himself a Genghis Khan or a Charlemagne. He likewise did not consider his coming encounter with Anatoly Gritchkin a major battle where wit and surprise and subterfuge would make the difference between victory and defeat. But he did plan for the worst, and he knew that he could not continue to assume that Gritchkin did not know of the twenty armed guards assigned to escort him to the airplane.

Carter could assume very little.

However, if his plan went according to the way he had mapped it out, the regular passengers for Flight 9 would arrive unexpectedly and throw the Russians off their guard, or put them on guard against a diversion so that he, Carter, could slip in easily and take the briefcase from Gritchkin while the guards would be trying to deal with an unruly and angry crowd of would-be passengers.

Once the Russians told the passengers that they couldn't board the aircraft, all hell would break loose. In that critical moment, the guards would be highly vulnerable. In that critical moment, the Killmaster would strike.

He had decided to try to shoot the handcuffs from Gritchkin's wrist with his Luger. Failing that, he would bring his stiletto into play and cut off the man's hand.

Carter had faith in his plan. He had only to remain out of sight and unnoticed until the passengers swarmed around the boarding tunnel, demanding entry to the plane. When Gritchkin and his guards tried to push through, Carter himself would start the rebellion among the passengers.

He was counting on their anger. In fact, when he had called the people on the list given him by the ticket agent, he had made certain that each person was properly angry about the much-delayed flight. He had played the part of Pushkin, with one major alteration in character. Instead of being unctuous and obliging, he had been nasty.

The passengers had objected to that, and to the short warning time. Carter, as Pushkin, had responded with more nastiness until all the passengers were ready to string him up. Unable to do so, they were ripe to take out their anger and frustration on the first person, or persons, to cross them.

And those persons, Carter figured, would be the guards at the gate who would deny the passengers access to Flight 9.

Carter was so wrapped up in his planning and in his anticipation of the scenes that would enfold at the airport that he didn't see the large car pull from a side street and move up behind him. When he saw the car, it was only a few feet behind and moving up fast as though the driver planned to ram the little VW Rabbit.

"Christ," Carter muttered. "Not another hit squad."

He speeded up, even though he knew it was fruitless to try to outrun the hog of a car that was practically on his tail. The big car kept pace, and as the Rabbit shot through a traffic circle, the bumpers touched. Carter felt the little car's rear tires skid sideways, then back and forth. This squad wasn't going to waste bullets, he realized. The men in the big car were going to smash him up like a giant trash compactor.

Carter was just snaking Wilhelmina from the snug holster under his arm when the car backed off and started another run at the VW Rabbit.

He checked to make certain the street ahead was straight and that no cars were in the way. He turned and aimed the Luger at a spot where the driver of the big car must be sitting. He was about to pull the trigger when the big car braked with a loud squeal of tires, then swerved to go around the Rabbit.

What the hell? Carter wondered.

As the other car eased alongside and Carter still held the Luger, he recognized the big Mercedes that Tammi Krisler drove. Damn, he thought, had the Soviets caught her, killed her, and taken her car?

And then he saw the driver smiling from ear to ear.

It was Tammi Krisler.

For a breathless instant, Carter thought the woman had indeed betrayed him. Memories of other women, so deeply trusted, who had betrayed and even tried to kill him were sharp in his mind.

But Tammi Krisler had no gun, and she was alone in the car. She motioned for Carter to pull over. *Well*, he thought as he put Wilhelmina back into the holster, *why the hell didn't she do this in the first place?* Why the dangerous game of bumper cars?

"Just what the hell do you think you're doing?" he demanded when they were both parked on a dark street and he had walked back to her car.

"I've tasted danger," Tammi said with a grin, "and I love it. Besides, you're always getting into car chases and playing bump-the-bumper. What's the big deal?"

"The big deal," Carter said, touching the bulge under his arm meaningfully, "is that you damned near got a nine-millimeter hunk of lead between the eyes. If you hadn't hit the brakes that last time, I would have drilled you."

"Oh, Nicholas," she chided, "must you be so melo-dramatic? I was only teasing you."

Carter grinned, but there was no mirth in the grin. It was

the look of a man who has known too much death and knows that it is no teasing matter. Carter hadn't lost his sense of humor. It was just that he had grown to really like this crazy girl and he had almost killed her. In that, he judged, there was no room for humor.

"Don't ever do such a thing again," he said sternly. "I mean it. Which brings up a question. Why are you here? I thought you were going to disappear for two hours and come back when your nest was put together again."

"I went away," she said, her lower lip sticking out in a lovely pout. "I went a whole block and parked behind a clump of bushes. I watched you go across to the Dussemann house and I watched you leave. I saw a van go into my driveway and assumed that it contained the men who will fix up my house and get rid of that Russian I shot. I followed you, and since you looked so vulnerable in that little trinket of a car, I decided to have some fun. Are you really angry at me, Nicholas?"

"No," Carter said, still regarding her grimly. "I'm furious. Didn't you hear what I said? I almost killed you. I was within a fraction of a second of pulling the trigger."

"You had a gun aimed at me?"

"I don't usually send out hunks of lead from my forefinger," Carter said, letting his facial muscles relax into a tight smile. "But enough of this. You told me what you've done, now tell me why you've done it. Why are you following me?"

"I wanted to tell you something important," Tammi said, her face bright and eager. "I was too brusque with you when I left the house. I'm sorry about that."

"You did all this just to tell me you're sorry that you were brusque?"

"No," Tammi said, her eyes looking away from Carter's penetrating gaze. "I came to tell you—well, let me put it this way, Nicholas. You're going to do something really foolish tonight. I don't know what it is, but I do know that you'll probably get yourself killed. I couldn't let you go thinking that I didn't care about you or what happens to you.'' She turned to look at him. Her large blue eyes were glistening with tears. ''Oh, Nicholas, I think I've really fallen in love with you. I know I've said I love you when we make love, but that's different. This is real and deep and enduring.''

Nick Carter was shaken all the way down to his toes. He realized with the suddenness of colliding trains why Tammi Krisler had played that dangerous game with him. She was convinced that he was going to be killed tonight and she loved him enough not to want to go on living without him. She had tried to provoke him into killing her but had changed her mind at the last minute.

No, Carter told himself, *that's not true.* He felt a moment of shame for being so presumptuous. Tammi had a great deal to live for. She had no idea of how dangerous her game was. If his ego hadn't got in the way, he wouldn't have thought otherwise.

''Didn't you hear me, Nicholas?'' Tammi said. ''Oh, you fool, don't you know why I played that silly game? I wanted you to shoot ı. ɔ with that big German gun of yours. I know you're going to die and I don't want to go on—''

''Stop it!'' Carter cried. ''Tammi, just stop it. I can take a lot from you, but I won't let you make bad jokes at my expense. You—''

Tammi was crying. Her long fingers covered her face and her shoulders shook with sobs as she sat behind the wheel of her big luxury car and let it out. Carter opened the door and nudged her until she moved over. He got in and closed the door, checking his watch to make certain he wasn't going to be late greeting Anatoly Gritchkin and his friends at Schiphol.

He took the lovely woman into his arms and let her cry on his shoulder. She cried for five minutes before the tears stopped and the sobs settled down to occasional sniffs, like hiccups. Carter couldn't believe what the woman had told him. She had voiced his actual thoughts, thoughts that he'd chided himself for having. But he believed her. And he thought he knew why she had acted the way she had.

Carter had opened up a whole different world for Tammi Krisler when he'd mentioned the possibility that relatives existed in East Germany, perhaps even in Dresden where her parents had been born. He had, in effect, destroyed the carefully constructed façade behind which the woman had been hiding for years. Tammi had known of her parents' life—they had told her. But that life was too horrible to contemplate. Tammi had built her own life, her own brand of security, and she was reasonably happy and safe in it. She was certainly successful. Carter had liked her from the moment he had walked into the Nieuw Gudens nightclub years ago and had heard her singing.

He didn't know then that the day would come when he would destroy Tammi Krisler's fragile world and make her want to die.

"Tammi, listen to me," he said when she was finally through crying. "You can't be in love with me any more than you could have grown up in Dresden. It just wasn't a part of your fate, your karma, your kismet—whatever you want to call it. Yes, I might die tonight. The odds are against me, if only because I've gone through far too many firefights and come out more or less victorious. If I don't get killed tonight, I'll get it some other night. If you tie your future to me, you won't have much of a future. And I don't want to hear anymore about you wanting to die or not being able to go on without me. You're made of sterner stuff than that. Just don't let yourself fall in love with me. Go out and find—''

''Too late,'' Tammi said, sniffling and hiccupping again. ''I said I thought I'd fallen in love with you, but that was an understatement. I *am* in love with you, Nicholas, and nothing in this whole wide world can ever change that. Now, don't preach to me. Just make love to me before you go off and get yourself killed.''

They crawled into the back seat, and although Carter was still woozy from the wound and the Demerol, he put that problem into the back of his mind. The back part of just about anything, he decided, was handy to have around.

Within a few moments of kissing and being kissed, of fondling and being fondled, Carter was in a state of bliss. He undressed Tammi in the back seat of that gorgeous car, and he kissed her lovely breasts and took her soft nipples into his mouth and felt her lips on his thighs and stomach. When they climaxed, together, the big car rocked with the vigor of their thrashing bodies, and Nick Carter could not have cared less, at that moment, about a spy named Anatoly Gritchkin and a briefcase full of data that could very well trigger World War III, a war that would annihilate the United States and its allies but leave the Soviet-bloc nations virtually untouched.

The black limousine was cruising down Rijksweg 4, past Schiphol Airport, heading for the center of Amsterdam. Anatoly Gritchkin had more than an hour and a half before the plane was to depart, and he knew that the plane would not leave without him. He was in no hurry.

The Soviet spy had work to do if his plan to eliminate the pesky American spy were to succeed.

The driver, a medium-level KGB agent, had objected when Gritchkin had ordered him to pass the airport and go directly into the city. But the driver hadn't heard the telephone conversation between Gritchkin and the chief; he knew none of the details of tonight's activities.

"Do as I tell you," Gritchkin had ordered grouchily. "Drive us to the Nederlands Hilton."

Now, well past the airport and heading into the city proper, Anatoly Gritchkin lifted the radiotelephone and pressed a series of buttons.

A voice responded and Anatoly Gritchkin asked a few questions, made a few suggestions, then hung up the radiophone. He sat back in the luxurious seat of the car he had borrowed from the Soviet ambassador to the Netherlands. He opened a fragrant Cuban cigar and lighted it with a gold lighter.

Ah, he would miss such luxuries once he was back in Moscow. Frankly, Anatoly Gritchkin didn't really want to go home. He knew that he was on his final assignment, that even though he should be given a hero's laurels and retired to a *dacha* on the Black Sea, he would instead be shamed by the presence of the guard contingent, retired to a desk in the KGB's central offices, and milked for everything he knew of the West.

That is, he thought as he puffed on the mellow cigar, he would be shamed and put behind a dull desk unless he took out the American agent who apparently was of very high level.

As he had been within a whisker of being killed by that damned American, he was now within a whisker of turning the tables.

Everything now hinged on the response to his radiophone contact with the Netherlands headquarters of the KGB. It was important that the operator with whom

Gritchkin had talked not speak of the spy's request with their mutual superior officers. If the man did as Gritchkin requested, consulted his computers quietly and efficiently, and came up with the proper answers, Anatoly Gritchkin would indeed return home a hero, minus the guard contingent. After suitable ceremonies in which he would be named Hero of the State, he would retire to that *dacha*, and he would live the high life for the remainder of his days.

Gritchkin had taken steps to make certain that the balance of his days, which would be few if the data in his briefcase were as important as he guessed, would be lived with special pleasure.

Oh, he would not enjoy the fine champagne and the class acts put on at places like Chez Carlo in Antwerp and Chez Paul in Brussels, but certain people in Russia managed to escape the life of boredom specified by the State. As a Hero, he would have tremendous licence to do much as he pleased.

Everything hinged on the reply from the radiophone operator at KGB headquarters in the Dutch city and on the success of Gritchkin's plan at the airport. The spy had a good feeling about both aspects of his plan, and when the radiophone light came on, he snatched the microphone from its hook with all the eagerness of a hungry gourmet going after snails in garlic butter.

"Gritchkin here," he blurted before he realized that he should have used his code name—there was no telling how many nosy amateurs were listening in on this frequency.

"I have your man," the operator said. "His name is Plotnick. He is assigned to a local section, but we should have no trouble borrowing him."

"You are certain that this man Plotnick fits the description?"

"The computer assures me that he does," the operator replied. "When the computer tells me something, I do not question it."

"All right. Give me Plotnick's home telephone number. I have no time to go through channels."

Gritchkin switched to the mobile telephone to call Plotnick. He identified himself by code, assured the man that he was making contact by authority of both their superiors, and ordered Plotnick to meet him in fifteen minutes at the Nederlands Hilton, Suite 2730. Plotnick began to protest.

"No time, comrade," Gritchkin snapped. "Be there in fifteen minutes or I will send a squad to eliminate you and your entire family from the face of the earth. Do you understand me, Comrade Plotnick?"

"Yes," Plotnick said, defeated. "Fifteen minutes. Suite Twenty-seven-thirty of the Nederlands Hilton. I shall be there."

Anatoly Gritchkin sat back again, more relaxed than he had been in days. He noticed that his cigar had gone out. To hell with it. He tossed out the long butt, lighted another beauty from Castro's island, and wondered just how long he could maintain his pipeline for Cuban cigars.

When he pulled off tonight's clever little coup, the pipeline would be open and flowing until the missiles began to fly.

Unfortunately, it would be impossible for the Soviet Union to destroy the continental United States without taking Cuba right along with it. Too bad. Gritchkin would miss those marvelous cigars.

FIFTEEN

Carter played head games all the way to the airport. The little engine whirred like a toy through the Amsterdam night, and the Killmaster also kept a wary eye out for bigger and meaner cars that might carry death squads. He had no problems on the highways. At the airport, he checked his watch and saw that he had an hour and twelve minutes before the plane was to depart.

In less than an hour, though, the passengers would arrive and pandemonium would reign near the gate from which Flight 9 was to depart.

Making no attempt to disguise himself, Carter left the VW Rabbit in the airport executives' parking lot where it could be extracted only with a special pass, and walked to a gate leading to the flight and taxiing areas. He leaped the gate and, eluding a sleepy guard, walked boldly out among the huge, lumbering aircraft parked at the many gates and linked to the terminal building by those long, concertinalike tubes.

Ten minutes later, he reached the Aeroflot departure area and saw the big Saroya, the spitting image of a Boeing 727, right where he had seen it last. He walked around the plane as though he were an airport executive making certain that all was going well with his airport.

Carter was surprised to find the aircraft still at the gate, and he was even more surprised to find that it wasn't guarded by a number of KGB types. Considering the amount of sabotage he had inflicted on Aeroflot's fleet, he expected heavy flak from KGB guards.

He walked casually around the aircraft and noted that the window he had shot out when he had almost killed Anatoly Gritchkin had been replaced. The escape chute had been deflated and repacked, the emergency door closed. And, Carter guessed, the problems he had created with his lethal little stiletto must have been corrected by Aeroflot's mechanics.

Only when he was certain that the master spy hadn't set a trap for Carter near the plane did he enter the terminal building. He went through the same doorway he had used when he had escaped from the plane during that ill-fated flight toward Moscow and back. He walked through stacks and stacks of luggage and packed boxes, and found the elevator to the top floor, the one for plane arrivals and departures.

He would start at the top, just in case Gritchkin had arrived early from his revelries in Antwerp and had laid his trap up there. Carter walked up and down the concourse from which Flight 9 would depart, then checked out the collateral concourses.

There were no signs of a trap.

At the Flight 9 gate there was no activity at all, not even a guard or airport employee to keep people from walking right into the boarding tube. Even so, Carter went on past, resisting the temptation to go aboard to find out if Gritchkin had again outwitted him and was already in his seat, grinning like a Cheshire cat. More likely, Carter thought, he'd run into a thick-headed, low-level KGB thug who would put a bullet in his chest and save the questions for later.

Convinced that the top floor was clean, Carter descended the big escalator to the floor where all the airlines had ticket counters and baggage check-in facilities. For as far as he could see down the long, wide concourse, passengers were standing in lines at one ticket counter after another. Schiphol was a very busy airport, even at this time of night. Such activity, he guessed, went on all night, and that was good. The more people around, the better his chances of getting to Gritchkin in a quick, surprise assault, and walking (or running) away with that briefcase that had already caused a great deal of trouble and many deaths.

Carter blended with the crowds, standing in one line after another. He was looking for something in particular and cursed himself for not thinking of his plan earlier, when the leather shops were open. Carter wanted a black briefcase, more or less similar to the one that Gritchkin had handcuffed to his wrist. If anyone—police especially—spotted him before and after the surprise assault he planned, he wanted those people to recall that he had carried a black briefcase all along.

It was also important, he decided, to carry a briefcase as a simple cover for his presence in the airport. Everyone carried something: briefcases, suitcases, valises, packages, purses. The man who carried nothing stuck out like a bandaged finger. Carter did carry his trench coat over one arm, but he still looked like a man who had no business in an airport.

In front of the Lufthansa counter, he found what he needed. A chunky German stood talking rapidly to a whole gaggle of people who had come to bid him bon voyage. The man's black briefcase was sitting on the floor near his legs. His luggage was on a wheeled carrier and being handled by a skycap. The briefcase, for the moment, was forgotten.

With hardly a ripple in his stride—and with barely a dip in his posture—Carter walked past the heavy German and snaked the briefcase from its place on the carpet. He kept on walking, expecting at any second to hear the German call out, then to hear the irritating *whee-oo, whee-oo* of a Dutch policeman's whistle.

Nothing happened. Carter moved on past Avianca Airlines, TWA, Qantas, and Swissair. When he neared the Aeroflot area, he moved to the opposite wall, and using the throng of passengers as shields, he surveyed the counter.

The man named Pushkin was there, busily explaining to would-be passengers that no Aeroflot flights were scheduled until further notice. Those scheduled (or that were supposed to be scheduled) on Flight 9 were not in attendance. They would come later, and they would go directly to the departure gate, thanks to Carter's tedious chore of telephoning.

Carter watched Pushkin and detected a note of arrogance, even nastiness, in his attitude toward passengers who assailed him with question after question. He puzzled over the man's obvious change in attitude, then grinned when he figured it out. The promise of ten thousand guilders had changed him. Carter had guessed right. The man accepted bribes because he was building a fund so that he could defect to the West. With the knowledge that he now had enough money to realize his dream, he had short patience with his employers who had put him in such a position with the passengers by canceling all flights. In turn, he had short patience with the passengers who kept annoying him with endless questions.

Carter moved on to check the main doors. Seeing nothing there, or outside, he checked the smaller entrances to the terminal. All was quiet. He saw no KGB types among the crowds.

Perhaps it was too early, he thought. He checked his watch again. The plane to Moscow was due to leave in forty-five minutes.

Convinced that the whole airport was clean for the moment, Carter dashed back down to the baggage area where he "borrowed" an electric cart laden with luggage from a Lufthansa flight. Nearby, several Lufthansa uniforms for baggage handlers hung on hooks. Carter chose one approximately his size, donned it and drove the cart onto a freight elevator. On the top floor, he backed the cart into a narrow alcove, took off the white coveralls, and put them on top of the luggage. With luck, he thought, it would all be here when he needed it—if he needed it. He hastened back to the main floor with his stolen briefcase.

Relaxing in a comfortable lounge chair near the main entrance, Carter flipped open a Dutch newspaper and pretended to read it.

He picked up on the head games he had played on the trip to the airport.

If I were Anatoly Gritchkin, he thought, *how would I arrive at Schiphol Airport knowing that an American agent has once nearly killed me and has killed several of my best men and is no doubt here waiting for me?*

There were many answers to that hypothetical question. Gritchkin could already be aboard that plane. Carter doubted it. The man had obviously been notified by his superiors that the plane would be ready to depart at a certain time, and the man just as obviously had received that word when he was enjoying the decadence of Chez Carlo in Antwerp. No, he wasn't aboard the plane.

Was he already in the airport, though, cruising around the way Nick Carter had been cruising around, looking for signs of the man who was on his trail? Was he right now watching Carter as he sat near the main entrance and pretended to read a newspaper?

And if he were, would Carter recognize him?

Carter had seen the man twice, but one of those occasions had been under very trying and nervous circumstances. He recalled the thatch of white hair, the heavyset body, and the bulging eyes. He recalled the man's sedate but very proper clothing, and his smooth, well-modulated voice. But he had observed all this in a state of high anxiety, when he was in danger of being killed, either by Gritchkin's bodyguards or by the thrashing plane. Could he trust those observations to be accurate?

Although Carter's mind continued the head games and mulled over every conceivable way in which Anatoly Gritchkin might return to the airport, no solution emerged. Carter was winging it all the way. Anything could happen, he told himself, and it probably would. Murphy's Law, in which anything that *could* go wrong *would* go wrong? Possibly.

He could only wait. He could only expect the unexpected.

It came sooner than he wanted it.

When it was thirty minutes until flight time, Tammi Krisler walked through the main entrance and stood gazing around as if trying to decide whether to go to Aeroflot's counter or to check the flight and gate numbers on one of the electronic monitors and go directly to the gate.

Carter was about to call to her, to get her off to some safe corner, when he saw two men enter the main door and step off to one side. They weren't watching Tammi specifically, but Carter knew from experience that they had her under surveillance.

Memories of that brief encounter with the beautiful Russian woman named Andrea Boritsky flooded his mind. Was Tammi working with the Russians the way Andrea had been? Was she here as part of some plan to sucker him? It was possible, he thought, that Gritchkin was having the same doubts Carter had about recognizing his adversary. Carter had seen Gritchkin twice, but the Russian had seen Carter only once.

And then it hit Carter. Tammi was not working with the Russians. They knew of her, had seen her with him. They had put a tail on her, and she had accommodated them by following Carter to the airport. When they had said good-bye, he had suspected that she might follow. Yet after he had been in the airport several minutes and she didn't show, he put that worry out of his mind.

Now she was here, and the minute she spotted him and came rushing over, he would become a bull's-eye for any number of KGB guns.

While Carter dealt with such thoughts, four more men came into the concourse and started up a conversation on the opposite side of the doorways from their comrades. Carter recognized them all by type: KGB all the way.

Carter raised the newspaper when Tammi Krisler scanned the lounge area where he sat. He hoped she wouldn't recognize his clothing. She apparently didn't, because she soon moved down the concourse. The six KGB types were close behind.

Carter waited, and sure enough, four more KGB goons came through the main doorway. He waited a few moments more and was ready to move to the mezzanine for a better vantage point when two more KGB men entered. Close behind them was Anatoly Gritchkin, the black briefcase handcuffed to his wrist. Behind Gritchkin were squads of KGB, moving in packs of two and four, flanking out around the master spy.

The Killmaster froze behind his newspaper, but his eyes never left the heavyset, white-haired man with the bulging eyes and the important briefcase. There was something about the way the man moved that troubled him, but he couldn't determine what. He tried to remember when he had watched Gritchkin's arrival from London, how the man had marched boldly along, berating those around him, being as pompous and overbearing as a man could be.

Gritchkin now seemed defeated, a man who walked with too many worries and burdens on his back, a man who was afraid of those around him and who concluded himself in a low-profile manner as if to avoid drawing attention to himself.

Well, it was no wonder, Carter thought. The man has been caught screwing around in nightclubs and has been ordered back to Moscow with a guard contingent. He had babysitters on this trip because he had failed on the first try and because he wasn't to be trusted. That, Carter guessed, was why he walked as though he were being led to the gallows.

The group with Gritchkin did not follow the group tailing Tammi Krisler. This group went instead to the escalator and began the smooth ride up past the mezzanine to the arrivals and departures level. They were going, Carter decided, directly to the gate where Flight 9 waited.

And then Carter saw someone else he recognized. When he had been aboard Flight 9, he had behaved badly on purpose in order to draw attention to the Dutch businessman he was portraying and to dissuade anyone from thinking that he was an American. When he had been at his worst, two German women on their way to Warsaw had openly commented on how disgusting the "Dutch- man" was.

Now those two women, followed by several other people Carter vaguely recognized, barged into the airport and made for the escalator.

Well, he thought, rising to follow, *now comes the moment of truth.* He headed for the staircase, knowing that he could beat the lot of them upstairs and to the gate.

He had decided that he would make his assault at the gate before Gritchkin could enter the boarding tube and when the passengers were at their angriest. But first, he knew, he had to delay Gritchkin long enough for the passengers to get the word that they were being denied entry to the aircraft.

As Carter sped along the upper concourse ahead of the two groups—the KGB guards with the spy, and the hope- ful passengers—he thought of Tammi Krisler and won- dered how she was making out with the six men who had followed her. When she failed to lead them to Carter, would the KGB agents let her alone, or would they decide to yank her into a men's room and cut her throat? Then again, the rankling thought came, she could be working for them. He refused to accept that.

Not a hundred feet from Flight 9's departure gate, Carter resurrected the electric baggage cart he had parked in an alcove. He pulled the tarp off the luggage, put on the white Lufthansa uniform, and waited for the KGB men and Anatoly Gritchkin.

He had a short wait.

Just as they rounded a group of departing passengers, Carter bolted forward in the cart and made a sharp right turn, away from the Russians. He kept his face averted, but he knew from the loud yell from the lead KGB man that his plan was working.

He had loosened the straps holding the luggage on the cart. When he made his sharp turn, all the suitcases began to tumble off in front of the Russian guards. He knew that he should keep on going, pretending that he hadn't noticed the spill, but he had to make certain that the angry passengers passed the Russians.

He backed up the cart, crashing into suitcases and scattering the KGB guards.

"You stupid lout!" one of the KGB men shouted in Russian as a big Gucci bag crunched into his shins.

"Beg pardon, beg pardon," Carter cried out in Dutch as he leaped from the seat of the cart and began to toss suitcases back onto the carrier. He swung wide, forcing the KGB men to back off or be struck in the face. "Please help me," he cried. "These bags must be aboard Flight Twenty-two in five minutes or I will lose my job."

Carter saw the passengers streaming around the halted Russians. He also saw that Gritchkin was standing alone against the wall. Incredibly, the KGB guards had responded to his plea for help.

They were putting the damned suitcases back on the cart!

No one was guarding the Soviet spy!

Carter was about to trigger the spring mechanism that would snap Hugo, his trusty stiletto, into his hand, when he smelled a rat. A Russian rat.

He was gazing intently at Anatoly Gritchkin and the spy was looking back at him. Yet there was no look of apprehension on the spy's face. The man had seen Carter on the initial journey of Flight 9. He had even pulled off the fake mustache that Carter had worn when he was pretending to be the obnoxious Hans Vandergaard.

Suddenly the pieces began to fit together.

Gritchkin did not recognize Carter because this man was not Gritchkin. If he were, the KGB guards would not dare leave him to his own devices while they piled suitcases back onto a cart to help a presumably stupid and careless baggage handler.

That slumping, listless walk. That woebegone look about the eyes and face that suggested a trip to the gallows. It all fit now.

This man looked like Gritchkin on the surface, but the inner man did not match. How the spy had come up with such a perfect look-alike, Carter had only a vague idea. Computers. God, they had done an incredible job and Carter had almost been fooled.

He had been on the verge of blowing his own cover by attacking a phony stand-in for Gritchkin to steal a briefcase that had no value whatsoever.

Carter began piling suitcases on the cart, thinking, working out a plan in his mind.

If this man were playing the part of Gritchkin and was wearing a briefcase handcuffed to his hand, then the real Gritchkin was probably walking around the airport at his ease.

The real Gritchkin would show up to board the plane after Carter had taken the bait and had been killed by this KGB guard contingent. As Carter worked and thought, he noticed that the KGB men were indeed keeping an eye on the phony Gritchkin, ready to spring into action if anyone went near him or attacked him. They would sacrifice the Gritchkin look-alike in order to catch Carter, just as they had sacrificed Colonel John Parnell and Andrea Boritsky and two low-level KGB men in London. Just as they had sacrificed that three-man hit squad near Antwerp.

Carter wouldn't take the bait.

When the cart was loaded and no one had attacked the phony Gritchkin, neither the KGB guards nor the spy's stand-in seemed to know what to do next. They merely stood in the concourse and gazed about warily.

Carter got aboard the cart and drove past the gate where Flight 9 was waiting. A hundred feet beyond, he pulled into a narrow alcove and got off. He shucked the white coveralls, took the briefcase he had stolen from the German downstairs, and turned to walk back to the Flight 9's gate.

He stopped dead in his tracks.

Approaching the gate where passengers were loudly complaining about not being allowed to board was none other than Tammi Krisler.

Behind her, close enough to breathe down her lovely neck, was the real Anatoly Gritchkin.

In seconds, they would enter the boarding tunnel and Nick Carter would be helpless to do anything to stop them.

SIXTEEN

Time seemed to stand still.

Nick Carter, convinced that all his plans and bravado had gone for nothing, looked wildly about for something—anything—to stop the Soviet spy from boarding that plane.

Beyond the crowd of milling, shouting, angry passengers, he spotted four Dutch policemen. Someone might have called them when the suitcases had been spilled.

Carter noticed something else that was important to him. Tammi Krisler was not a willing companion to the Soviet spy. Gritchkin had her arm twisted behind her back. In her eyes was a look of absolute terror.

But a more vital observation came when an earlier suspicion was confirmed.

The briefcase that Anatoly Gritchkin carried in his right hand was not handcuffed to his wrist!

When the master spy had made the switch with the look-alike, he apparently had only one handcuff, or he decided that he no longer needed a handcuff—indeed, that it would single him out as a carrier of vital data.

Quickly, almost haphazardly, Carter formed a new plan in his mind. It was daring, bold, and dangerous. It was also simple, and Carter favored simple plans, especially if they worked.

Then another incredible development unfolded to aid his cause. Anatoly Gritchkin, instead of entering the boarding tunnel with Tammi Krisler and the KGB goons accompanying them, stopped to talk to the harassed boarding agent. He began to try to soothe the angry passengers, all the while gazing around as though looking for someone.

Carter knew who that someone was. He knew now just what Gritchkin had planned. The master spy would have had Carter killed in the trap set up by the man who looked like Gritchkin. Failing that, he wouldn't board the aircraft until he was certain that Carter was dead.

The spy, on the very edge of escaping Nick Carter forever, was unwilling to leave until the American who had been dogging his trail had been dispatched.

The police now moved toward the counter set up for the boarding agent, and Carter reassessed his views as to why the Dutch police were there. One of the passengers must have called the police, demanding justice. It didn't matter. His plan included using the police and he was just grateful that they were here.

Gripping the briefcase he had stolen from the chunky German, Carter marched down the concourse directly toward the melee being created by the angry passengers.

He headed toward Anatoly Gritchkin and Tammi Krisler, watching the movements of the police, timing his arrival with theirs.

As he neared the heavyset, white-haired spy who was smiling and trying to appease the passengers—and still holding Tammi's arm behind her back—Carter made his decision about how to involve the police. His initial thought had been to claim that the Russian was kidnapping a Dutch woman, but the Russians might have cooked up some ''proof'' that Tammi was indeed an East German who had defected. The Dutch did not grant political asylum the way the Americans and certain other Western European countries did. In asylum cases, the person usually headed for Belgium or England before declaring his intentions.

The briefcase was the answer, as it had been all along. Carter was just grateful that Gritchkin's briefcase was no longer handcuffed to his wrist. He could thank the ploy involving the look-alike for that fact.

''One moment!'' he cried out loudly in Dutch as he rushed toward Gritchkin. ''That man stole my briefcase!''

It was more than a simple plan; it was downright thin, Carter realized. But he needed any ruse to delay Flight 9 and Gritchkin's entry aboard that plane. The efficient Dutch police might not involve themselves in political asylum cases, but they were great on traffic offenses and theft—even alleged theft.

Gritchkin, Tammi, and the police turned as one person. Gritchkin and Tammi recognized Nick Carter at the same time. Gritchkin looked triumphant, convinced that the stupid American spy had walked directly into his clutches after having escaped a number of cleverly laid traps. Tammi was looking fearful, as though Carter's presence would get them both killed.

The police, on the other hand, were glancing at the briefcase in Gritchkin's hand and at the one in the accuser's.

Carter could virtually read the minds of the police. Perhaps, they thought, these two men had inadvertently taken each other's briefcases and one of them had discovered the switch. The police also had determined that there was nothing they could do to resolve the revolt or complaints of the passengers demanding access to Flight

9, and they seemed happy to be diverted by a problem they could handle.

Gritchkin, seeing the interested eyes of the police, looked beyond the crowd for help. Although he had a few bodyguards with him, his main guard contingent was on the fringe of the crowd, waiting with the befuddled man who had played the part of Gritchkin and had failed. The Russian spy, Carter could see, was worried. Gritchkin also knew of the efficiency of the Dutch police and knew that they wouldn't let either Gritchkin or the American spy out of their clutches until the matter of the briefcase was resolved. Gritchkin, Carter assessed, was highly pissed off.

The master spy from Moscow would have to endure this ridiculous claim from the master spy from Washington.

"That man," Carter explained in Dutch to the keenly interested policemen, "took my briefcase while I was standing at the Lufthansa ticket counter. Several of my family saw him take it, leave his own briefcase in exchange, and disappear into the crowd."

Two of the policemen nodded and explained to the two others that, indeed, there was a report of a stolen briefcase from the vicinity of the Lufthansa counter. The thief had not been caught, but it was their understanding that the man from whom the briefcase was stolen was German.

Carter, who had understood this exchange (although Gritchkin had not), responded in perfect German.

"Yes, I am German, but I spoke in your language to facilitate matters."

"Ah, good," the policeman with the most stripes on his uniform sleeve responded. He was, Carter determined, a lance corporal, equal to a squad leader on an American metropolitan police force. "And you are Herr Menschken?"

"*Ja*," Carter replied. "And I do not know who this

Russian gentleman is. I only know that my cousins said that the man who took my briefcase was a heavy man with white hair and bulging eyes. And that"—he pointed directly at the briefcase that Gritchkin held—"is my briefcase. I would recognize it anywhere. This one," he added, holding up the real stolen case, "was left in its place."

Carter noticed that Gritchkin was sweating. The man had no full knowledge of either Dutch or German, but he had caught the drift of the conversation.

The Russian spy was looking frantically past the crowd of angry passengers for Flight 9, but the members of his large guard contingent still hadn't tumbled to what was happening at the boarding gate.

"Well, gentlemen," the squad leader of the four Dutch policemen said, rapping each briefcase with a short baton he carried as a sign of rank (batons were optional, Carter knew), "we shall have to step across the concourse to the lounge area of the next gate. It is not occupied. There, we can ascertain just whose briefcase is whose."

During this exchange, Gritchkin had released his hold on Tammi Krisler's arm. The woman, sensing that Carter had some grand plan up his sleeve, did nothing to divert attention from the argument over the briefcase. But she did glance at Carter with a look of thanks and began to edge away from Gritchkin and his KGB friends. There were six of them, the same six that had followed Tammi Krisler into the airport.

Carter was grateful for that look. It spoke volumes. He tried to give her a look of reassurance in return, but she surely knew that he had doubted her at one point and now fully trusted her again. The girl was playing it cool, and convinced that something dramatic and dangerous was about to take place, she was moving away. But she stopped just past the boarding agent's counter and stood watching from behind a column.

Dammit, Carter thought. *Why doesn't she just keep on moving? If I get out of this alive, I can meet her downstairs, or out in the parking lot. Anywhere but here.* Already, the goons guarding Anatoly Gritchkin were moving their hands toward weapons concealed beneath their jackets.

Carter, in turn, was ready to pull Wilhelmina from her holster at any hint of a threat.

"You will please come with us," the Dutch corporal said to Gritchkin in rather shabby Russian. "We must determine—"

"Nyet!" Gritchkin cried loudly in Russian. "I am going no place! This man is an imposter! He is not a German. He is an American spy sent to steal important Soviet documents from me. I will not tolerate any interference. I will now board my flight to Moscow, and I will not submit to any delay by stupid Dutch pigs."

It was, Carter thought, the worst thing Gritchkin could have said to the proud policeman with the stripes. As for himself, he was delighted that Gritchkin had said it. Even so, the lance corporal was the soul of patience and diplomacy.

"It will take but a few minutes," he said. "Once the truth is ascertained, and if it is determined that your claim is true, you will be free to leave. You have ample time to catch your flight, because it does not depart for—"

He got no further.

All hell broke loose.

Gritchkin, who carried no weapon, suddenly reached into the jacket of the KGB man nearest him and brought out a wicked-looking .45 automatic pistol. He had shifted the briefcase to his left hand and was now pointing the gun directly at the policemen, waving it back and forth.

"Go away!" he ordered as he began to back up toward the boarding tunnel. "Just go away and leave me alone! I am a Russian diplomat and have important Soviet material in this briefcase. I will not be delayed by stupid Americans and stupid Dutch."

Carter had already responded to the threat Gritchkin represented. He was moving quickly toward the Soviet spy. He had dropped the stolen briefcase and was going for two things: to kill Gritchkin, and to get that briefcase filled with America's White Horse space weaponry data.

The remaining five KGB men with Gritchkin were also responding. They had their weapons out. Instead of aiming at Carter, they were aiming at the Dutch police who, except for the lance corporal, were already halfway to the empty lounge across the concourse.

The five KGB men fired as one, literally blowing the lance corporal apart.

The sound of gunfire panicked the angry passengers who had been demanding access to Flight 9. Screams resounded up and down the concourse. The three Dutch policemen who had watched their leader go down were snatching pistols from their buttoned holsters.

Carter pounded into Gritchkin, knocking him backward and sending a number of innocent passengers sprawling.

"Get out of here!" he cried to the crowd. "Don't you understand? There will be no flight! Just go!"

In that instant, he was sorry that he had called the passengers and put them in such jeopardy. But they had been a help; there was no doubt of that. The only trouble was, their usefulness had ended and now they were in danger.

Carter didn't waste a moment with Gritchkin this time.

When he had slammed into the man, he had knocked the .45 automatic from the spy's hand. Now Carter had Hugo in his palm, and moving swiftly, he cut Gritchkin's throat. The huge bulging eyes only bulged more as the Russian died in a cascade of his own blood.

The Killmaster snatched the black briefcase. As he closed his hand on the sweaty handle, he heard new gunfire erupt behind him. The KGB men and the three remaining Dutch policemen were shooting it out.

Carter decided to put Wilhelmina to work. He quickly returned his stiletto to its sheath and unholstered the Luger. He took careful aim at the wide back of one KGB man and squeezed the trigger.

The boom of the big Luger was the crowning glory of the wild sounds in the concourse. Carter caught a sideways glimpse of passengers fleeing for their lives, but his real interest was in the KGB man ahead of him. He could see the small bullet hole in the back of the man's jacket, yet the man was standing still, as though nothing had happened.

Slowly, as in a nightmare, the KGB man turned and his legs began to buckle beneath him. As his body turned toward Carter, the man from AXE saw the results of the 9mm slug that had hurtled from the muzzle of Wilhelmina.

The entire front of the Russian's shirt was soaked in blood. The shirt was shredded, and Carter could see flesh and bone protruding, could see blood pumping from a severed artery.

That was the nasty thing about close shots, even with a Luger. The hole going in was always small. The hole coming out was almost always wide and jagged and wicked-looking.

Carter picked out a second KGB man, drilled him twice, and swung to a third. As he was squeezing the trigger, the man flew backward and Carter saw that a Dutch policeman, the only one he saw still standing, had just hit the KGB agent with a chest shot.

Carter and the policeman each dispatched another KGB man, leaving only one alive, the one whose weapon Gritchkin had taken. The man had somehow blended into the crowd, but he had apparently taken a fallen weapon with him.

Gunfire erupted from the fleeing passengers, and Carter saw the tongue of flame from a handgun.

For one terrible moment, a millisecond and no more, he was convinced that the onrushing death missile was for him. He prepared for pain and death.

But the slug hit the remaining Dutch policeman squarely between the eyes. Carter took careful aim at the gunman, was about to fire, and decided against it. The slug from Wilhelmina could easily go astray and kill a passenger.

If any innocent people are to die today, he thought, *let it be on the backs of the Russians.*

Most of the passengers were now fleeing toward the main concourse. Carter saw no sign of the main guard contingent that had been with Gritchkin's look-alike. He looked around wildly, and sure enough, there was Tammi Krisler. She had moved behind the thick column, out of the way of the gunfire. The boarding agent had disappeared into the boarding tube.

"Come on!" Carter said, rushing up to grab Tammi's hand. "Let's catch up with the passengers and leave with them. It's our only chance."

"My God, what a sight!" Tammi gasped as Carter pulled her away from the scene of death at the gate. "I

knew you lived with violence, Nicholas, but this is bar-
baric.''

"That it is. Let's get away from here before it gets even
worse."

They hadn't gone more than fifty feet when Carter
spotted the first KGB man waiting for them in a narrow
alcove, the one in which he had parked the baggage cart.
And then the concourse, rapidly emptying as passengers
from all gates fled the bloody scene, seemed to be filling
with grim-faced KGB types with pistols in their hands.

Carter and Tammi stopped. Carter assessed the situation ahead and knew that it was hopeless. They were
trapped.

"Come this way!" he said, turning with Tammi's hand
still gripped in his.

"But, Nicholas," she protested, "this concourse ends
just around the next corner! We'll be trapped there!"

"We're trapped now," he yelled. "Let's move it!"

They literally stepped over the sprawled bodies of
Gritchkin, the five KGB men, and the three Dutch
policemen. Carter felt deep remorse for the deaths of the
innocent policemen. He had known that something violent might happen when he had tried that dangerous ploy
with the briefcases, but he really hadn't expected any of
the Russians to open fire on the local police.

In the game of spying, Carter knew, that was a definite
taboo. When spies of two nations operated on neutral soil,
they were scrupulously careful not to ruffle the feathers of
the authorities of that neutral territory. The repercussions
would be devastating for other spies in the future. The
Dutch might even decide to keep out Americans and
Russians alike, innocent or guilty.

Carter found the electric baggage cart and hopped into
the driver's seat. Tammi leaped aboard and sat beside

him. He whizzed out of the narrow alcove just as a dozen KGB guards went to a kneeling position a hundred feet away and prepared to fire at them.

The thunder of gunshots, all coming simultaneously, nearly burst their eardrums. Carter heard the slugs tearing into the suitcases behind them. He floored the pedal, but the cart moved only about as fast as a man could comfortably run.

And then, as more thunder of gunfire rumbled up and down the concourse, Carter saw the end wall and knew that he had to make his stand. He had one Luger against perhaps fifteen or twenty KGB men, all furious now that plans had gone awry and their master spy was dead and the briefcase that was the cause of it all was in the hands of the American.

Time, Carter knew, was of the essence. Dutch police would arrive soon in great force. They would take out the KGB men at great loss to their own ranks, but they would also have Carter and Tammi in custody. Carter could easily lose control over the briefcase and its contents.

As he pulled the electric cart into position across the end of the concourse and he and Tammi leaped behind the suitcases for protection, Carter glanced out the window. There was a short drop to a roof below, then a longer drop to the macadam. They would have to chance it if they had the opportunity.

Meanwhile, he waited for the KGB men to move up. He had to take out as many as possible before the Dutch police arrived. He wanted no more killing of innocent people.

Carter jammed a new clip into the Luger and handed it to Tammi. She stared at the lethal weapon as though it were something filthy from some strange garbage can. Carter opened his belt, dropped his trousers, and ripped the tape off Pierre, the tiny gas bomb on his thigh.

"Don't shoot unless some of them rush us before I can use this little treasure," he told Tammi. "If anyone survives, I'll take over the gun duties and pick off the stragglers."

"My God, you're like a killing machine!" Tammi wailed.

"Yeah," Carter said, recalling his reaction years ago when he had been accredited a Killmaster for AXE. "A killing machine. And there are a whole bunch of killing machines moving up that concourse to do us dirt. Keep your eyes dead ahead and keep your finger on the trigger."

Tammi's hand was shaking on the Luger, and Carter knew that she was about to fall apart. He had to keep her talking.

"How did Gritchkin get you?" he asked. "I thought you were going to hang around and go home when the place was fixed up."

"I did drive around for a time," Tammi said, "then I saw these men in a black limousine and I remembered something you had once said on the telephone. That a Russian spy was using the ambassador's car. I recognized the car as the Russian ambassador's from the diplomatic plates. I followed it and they saw me and they set a trap and caught me."

"I get the picture," Carter said. "But what about that charade downstairs, when you came in looking for me?"

"They sent me in alone," she said, "to spot you for them. They said they'd kill me if I didn't point you out. They were right behind me, Nicholas, and I didn't know if they meant business or not."

"They meant business," Carter said. "And that gang moving down the concourse also means business. How many do you count?"

They both took a count and came out the same. Sixteen men, all in a bunch, with two men lagging fifty feet behind.

They all carried guns, some of them AK-47 assault rifles. And they were moving swiftly, like a well-trained military squad. Some would die, they seemed to be saying, but some would survive to kill Carter and the girl, and to retrieve the briefcase taken from Comrade Gritchkin.

Carter felt a sickness in the pit of his stomach. He knew he couldn't get them all. Not even Pierre was that good. Not in that open a space. One thing was in his favor. The men were all bunched together, which would make the gas bomb's job a little easier.

There was another thing in his favor. He hadn't yet heard the irritating squeal of a Dutch policeman's whistle. With luck, this would all be over before the efficient cops arrived.

''Nicholas, they've started to rush us!'' Tammi cried.

She was gripping the pistol and actually aiming it at the onrushing team of KGB men. Carter pulled the pin on Pierre and lobbed the little gas bomb over the suitcase-laden cart.

Shots rang out and more bullets poured into the suitcases, and Carter wondered just whose suitcases these were and how the owners would react when they finally retrieved them and found their clothing full of lead and copper bullets.

There was a loud *poof* as the gas bomb went off. Carter and Tammi drew in deep breaths, just in case. They heard gasping and knew that men were dropping likes flies. Tammi dropped the Luger and put her hands to her mouth, as though to keep herself from throwing up.

Carter raised his head above the suitcases and saw that it was all over. The sixteen men up close were all dead. The two men lagging behind had seen them die, and they were turning now to run away. Discretion, Carter knew, was still the better part of valor.

And then came the irritating sound of *whoo-ee, whoo-ee*. The Dutch police were on their way.

Carter took a suitcase from the cart and used it to smash out a window at the end of the concourse.

"Come on, Tammi. We have no more business here."

They had no trouble making the two leaps to the ground. And they didn't look back when the Dutch police whistled at them from the broken window. They made straight for the executive parking lot, where Carter fired up the little VW Rabbit, drove it through the barrier set up to stop those who didn't have a special pass, and headed for the highway that would take them to the exclusive Buitenveldert section.

Carter was eager for a shower, and then he wanted to try out Tammi Krisler's new bed and he hoped that Hawk had remembered to specify pink sheets to the team that had come to take away the body of Josef Petrosky and to clean up the mess that had been made and then he would call Hawk and report that everything was just fine and. . . .

"Nicholas?" Tammi said as the little Rabbit hopped along, putting Schiphol and all that death behind.

"Yes?"

"I want you to know that I really do love you."

"I know."

"But I don't think I could live with you. Even for a year. Now I know what you'd be going back to, and I couldn't stand it. Is that okay?"

Carter grinned and drove faster. He was almost certain that Hawk wouldn't leave out an important item like pink sheets.

DON'T MISS THE NEXT NEW
NICK CARTER SPY THRILLER

THE NORMANDY CODE

They walked for nearly twenty minutes, around the quay and along the narrow canals leading inland from the harbor.

Carter stayed close to her, ready to put the arm on her if she bolted. Either she was legit, or she was out to con him for a thousand. The francs he wouldn't mind losing, but he didn't want to waste a lot of time going through the bar routine again.

"There."

Carter followed her pointing finger to a short, narrow barge bobbing in the canal.

"You're not coming on board?"

"No. His name is Pepe. Give me the other half of the thousand-franc note."

"Not until I come back."

She tossed him another French shrug, sat on a tie-up post, and lit a cigarette.

Carter jumped to the deck of the barge and moved aft to the hatch that led belowdecks. It was closed. He knocked, waited, and knocked again.

"Oui?"

"Pepe?"

"Oui . . ."

The hatch burst open, and before Carter could spring back, two hamlike hands had filled themselves with the front of his sweater. He was yanked from his feet, whirled, and thrown completely across the cabin against the far bulkhead.

He didn't slide clear to the deck, but almost.

"Are you police, *monsieur? . . . Sûreté? . . .* Interpol?"

The Killmaster gasped some air back into his lungs and shook his head to clear it. When his eyes focused, he saw the scarfaced fisherman looming above him, fists knotted, ready.

"No, I am an American."

"American police?"

"No. You know Serena?"

"I know the gypsy woman. She is a friend. That is why Pepe wants to know who you are."

"My name is Carter. If you can contact her, just tell her that Carter must see her."

"What about?"

"I can only tell her that myself."

"No, you must tell Pepe."

"I can't do that," Carter replied, using his heels on the deck to push himself upright.

"Then Pepe will have to beat the shit out of you."

He rushed, head pulled into his shoulders, both forearms up, fists only inches apart. Carter relaxed and took the surge like a wrestler, turning his body to the side at the last second.

The left was already jabbing. Carter caught the wrist

with his left hand and threw his right shoulder into the man's face.

Pepe stumbled and both of them went down, making kindling of a table in the process.

The guy was big, and probably an experienced barroom fighter. Carter had Hugo, but he didn't want to go that far. Once the stiletto came into the open, the Killmaster knew he would probably have to use it.

He wanted Pepe alive.

Pepe, his left wrist still locked in Carter's left hand, tried a high, wild right to the Killmaster's jaw. Carter rolled and nailed the scarred face again with his shoulder.

This time, the connection was solid. Bone and cartilage gave, and blood squirted like a geyser from the big man's nose and lips.

Carter was about to bring a knee into action, when Pepe got his left arm free. At the same time, he used his superior weight to roll up over the Killmaster.

A left rocked the side of Carter's jaw. He saw bloodred stars, then the right coming straight down as a follow-up.

He rolled his head to the side, felt the fist rake his ear, and then heard an agonizing scream of pain from the man above him.

Pepe had smashed his fist into the hardwood deck by Carter's head. At least three—and probably all—of his knuckles were broken.

He didn't know it, but it was the blow that lost him the fight.

—From THE NORMANDY CODE
A New Nick Carter Spy Thriller
From Charter in July 1985

NICK CARTER

☐ 74965-8	SAN JUAN INFERNO	$2.50
☐ 79073-9	THE STRONTIUM CODE	$2.50
☐ 82726-8	TURKISH BLOODBATH	$2.25
☐ 14220-6	DEATH ISLAND	$2.50
☐ 95935-0	ZERO-HOUR STRIKE FORCE	$2.50
☐ 03223-0	ASSIGNMENT: RIO	$2.50
☐ 14222-2	DEATH HAND PLAY	$2.50
☐ 29782-X	THE GOLDEN BULL	$2.50
☐ 45520-4	THE KREMLIN KILL	$2.50
☐ 52276-9	THE MAYAN CONNECTION	$2.50
☐ 10561-0	CIRCLE OF SCORPIONS	$2.50
☐ 06861-8	THE BLUE ICE AFFAIR	$2.50
☐ 51353-0	THE MACAO MASSACRE	$2.50
☐ 69180-3	PURSUIT OF THE EAGLE	$2.50
☐ 24089-5	LAST FLIGHT TO MOSCOW	$2.50
☐ 86129-6	THE VENGEANCE GAME	$2.50

Prices may be slightly higher in Canada.

Available at your local bookstore or return this form to:

CHARTER BOOKS
Book Mailing Service
P.O. Box 690, Rockville Centre, NY 11571

Please send me the titles checked above. I enclose _____ Include 75¢ for postage and handling if one book is ordered; 25¢ per book for two or more not to exceed $1.75. California, Illinois, New York and Tennessee residents please add sales tax.

NAME _____

ADDRESS _____

CITY _____ STATE/ZIP _____

(allow six weeks for delivery.)   A8